DEDICATION

For Grandma Sharon
I miss you.

Hunted in Darkness

AN ASPEN PACK NOVEL

CARRIE ANN RYAN

Hunted in Darkness
An Aspen Pack Novel
By: Carrie Ann Ryan
© 2022 Carrie Ann Ryan
eBook ISBN: 978-1-947007-50-5
Paperback ISBN: 978-1-947007-51-2

Cover Art by Sweet N Spicy Designs

PRAISE FOR CARRIE ANN RYAN....

"Count on Carrie Ann Ryan for emotional, sexy, character driven stories that capture your heart!" – Carly Phillips, NY Times bestselling author

"Carrie Ann Ryan's romances are my newest addiction! The emotion in her books captures me from the very beginning. The hope and healing hold me close until the end. These love stories will simply sweep you away." ~ NYT Bestselling Author Deveny Perry

"Carrie Ann Ryan writes the perfect balance of sweet and heat ensuring every story feeds the soul." - Audrey Carlan, #1 New York Times Bestselling Author

"Carrie Ann Ryan never fails to draw readers in with passion, raw sensuality, and characters that pop off the page. Any book by Carrie Ann is an absolute treat." – New York Times Bestselling Author J. Kenner

"Carrie Ann Ryan knows how to pull your heart-strings and make your pulse pound! Her wonderful Redwood Pack series will draw you in and keep you reading long into the night. I can't wait to see what comes next with the new generation, the Talons. Keep them coming, Carrie Ann!" –Lara Adrian, New York Times bestselling author of CRAVE THE NIGHT

"With snarky humor, sizzling love scenes, and brilliant, imaginative worldbuilding, The Dante's Circle series reads as if Carrie Ann Ryan peeked at my personal wish list!" – NYT Bestselling Author, Larissa Ione

"Carrie Ann Ryan writes sexy shifters in a world full of passionate happily-ever-afters." – *New York Times* Bestselling Author Vivian Arend

"Carrie Ann's books are sexy with characters you can't help but love from page one. They are heat and heart blended to perfection." *New York Times* Bestselling Author Jayne Rylon

Carrie Ann Ryan's books are wickedly funny and deliciously hot, with plenty of twists to keep you guessing. They'll keep you up all night!" USA Today Bestselling Author Cari Quinn

"Once again, Carrie Ann Ryan knocks the Dante's Circle series out of the park. The queen of hot, sexy, enthralling paranormal romance, Carrie Ann is an

author not to miss!" *New York Times* bestselling Author
Marie Harte

HUNTED IN DARKNESS

The Aspen Pack series from NYT Bestselling Carrie Ann Ryan continues with a fated romance that was never supposed to happen.

Skye Jamenson-Anderson knows the legacy she must live up to. She's the daughter of warriors and the granddaughter of the late Alphas who sacrificed everything so their den could survive. Though she feels she doesn't have a place in her Pack, she does everything in her power to keep them and their allies alive—including saving the Aspen Alpha.

As Alpha of the Aspen Pack, Chase Leyne knows a thing or two about one's legacy. He's the son of a traitor and the most powerful wolf in his territory. He also knows without a doubt that Skye is not his mate. When the two decide to lean on another in every way possible, they both go in knowing nothing forever can come out of it.

The enemy is stepping up their game and threaten the stability of the alliance forged in blood. With one bite, Chase and Skye's world changes, and the one thing that is keeping them apart might be the only promise to save their Packs and their future.

CHAPTER
ONE

Chase

W{\small HILE} I {\small WOULD}'{\small VE} {\small PREFERRED} {\small MY} {\small PAWS} {\small TO} {\small TOUCH} the ground, for the dirt to sink in between my toes as I leapt over a fallen log and wound between the trees, I needed to be human for this. I had to go back and meet with the council, as well as a visiting Beta. There were things to do with an upcoming war on the horizon, like the fact that we wouldn't be able to hide the vampires from the humans for much longer. As it was, we were certain that the government already knew something was changing. How had the vampires hidden for so long

—at least thirty years from what I could tell—and were now rolling out so quickly?

They were doing this for a reason.

That worried me.

Because we weren't ready, we were barely rising from the ashes as it was, but we needed to be better than this. We needed to focus and push through.

And that meant I needed to be at the top of my game.

I needed to stop with the nightmares. I needed to sleep through an entire night without waking up in a cold sweat, the feel of silver and metal against my back as I screamed in agony. I shouldn't have those dreams any longer.

I couldn't.

I had to be the Alpha the Aspens deserved.

I jumped over another log, my wolf at the forefront. He was pacing, eager for a hunt, but I knew it wasn't time yet. We would go on a hunt for the full moon in the coming days with the rest of the Pack. They would wait for me, and I would lead them.

They needed me to be their leader.

I had been the Heir who hadn't been allowed to be that person for so long. I'd been hidden away and hadn't saved my people.

But now I would lead them, and I would protect them.

There wasn't another choice.

I leapt over another log and kept going, annoyed with myself for letting the gloom hit me. I had so much energy, this rage that had been beaten and hidden within me for the years I was caged and locked away.

I still remembered Audrey's screams when she had been tortured next to me, stabbed over and over again in places that wouldn't damage any organs, but would still hurt her. We had been caged together, metal separating us, and I hadn't been able to save my best friend.

And she hadn't even known I was alive there.

The world had thought I was dead, hidden, but I had been there.

Somehow, I had survived. Maybe not whole, but enough.

I needed to survive.

I needed to protect my Pack.

I turned the corner, heading back to the den. They needed me, and while Steele didn't appreciate the fact that I was running alone, I was still within the den's reach. Anybody could get to me in less than five minutes. But I was an Alpha, and I could hold my own.

Far more than most people thought.

The first scent hit me, and my wolf went on alert as I slowed.

The moment I turned the corner, they moved.

As if they had been waiting.

3

Oh, they had known where I would be. They had to have. But how? How had they known?

I looked around, searching.

Vampires slid out of the darkness, but they were not overcome with blood hunger. No, these were sentient, with angry red eyes and immaculate control.

And they were waiting.

For me.

As they circled me, my claws slid out of my fingertips. I wouldn't have time to change into my wolf form, even though I was faster than most.

No, I would have to fight as human.

A wolf howled to the moon behind me, so close that I could scent her, and I hoped she would be quick enough.

Because I knew who was coming for me.

Who was going to try to save me.

I just didn't know if she would make it in time.

When the first vampire sliced at me, far quicker than any other vampire I had seen, I took the cuts to the arm with its claw, evading its fangs, and wondered if this was my end.

And then the rest of the vampires lunged, and I could think of nothing else.

I ducked out of the way of the closest black-tipped talon-like nails. My wolf pushed at me, coming to the surface.

My eyes glowed gold, the dominance of my animal far more than the vampire in front of me. It didn't matter that this looked to be one of the most sentient and powerful vampires I had ever seen. I was going to defeat him and all his little buddies.

Though their red eyes were narrowed into slits, they were still sentient. This one wasn't the type who rampaged and was without thought or intelligence. No, this one had the power to make decisions even if they weren't the one in full control. I ducked the next swipe, hooked my hand, claws out, and sliced through the belly of the closest vampire. As the creature let out a startled shout I reached up, my hand covered in blood, and twisted the thing's neck. It fell to the ground, twitching, before I went at another vampire.

One of them came at me, fangs bared. I slammed my hand into its throat and it staggered back. I twisted, going at another just as one of the damn vampires slid its fangs into my flesh. I half-shouted, half-howled, as I pried the vamp's mouth off me and twisted its neck. It fell into a dead heap of flesh at my feet.

Venom sliced through my veins, and I cursed. I knew this couldn't turn me, not from what we'd learned so far, but I didn't know if it could weaken me. I needed to get to my Healer so Wren could work the poison out of my system.

We honestly didn't know what happened to wolves

or other shifters once a vampire bit into them. We only knew that like turning a human into shifter, it took near death to turn a human into a vampire. That's what we had gleaned from the vampire general and his cronies like the dead Jagger. That vampire had killed himself rather than answer our questions.

My arm throbbing, my body radiating with tension, I came at the other vampire. One jumped onto my back, more vampires coming out of the woods, and I had to hope the fight was making enough noise that the Aspens on duty would come. I could damn well take these, bite notwithstanding, I just didn't want anybody to get hurt because of me.

Not again.

Before I could twist to tear the vampire off of my back, a silver bullet shot past me. Not the weapon, but a small wolf, not too dominant, but not submissive either.

Skye ripped the vampire off my back, growled, and tore into its neck, twisting its head off its body. I ducked the claw of another vampire and then Skye and I were working as a team, the two of us fighting off the vampires as if we had been fighting against our enemies side by side for generations, rather than the single other battle we had ever fought together.

Considering none of the Aspens on patrol had come yet, the vampires had to be using their magic to keep others from getting through their personal wards.

Because my sentries would be here—hell, my Enforcer, Steele, would be here if they could hear what was happening. Someone had known where I would be tonight and was making damn sure no one would be able to get to me.

It was just the two of us, and I was grateful Skye seemed to have been within the barrier of magic when the attack came. That was the only way she could have been through the vampire magic which seemed to be stronger than the shifters and witches combined.

It worried me because we did not have the coven's support, as the coven did not have the magic needed to protect us. Nor did the shifters have the same connections to this demon that the vampires did. There were either witches working with the vampires, or demon magic was stronger and worked in different ways than we had ever seen before. Either way, we needed to find a way to become stronger in magic.

I couldn't think of that right then. No, that was something for the Alpha part of me to work on later. Not the wolf part that needed to keep Skye and me safe. And that wasn't only because she was the daughter of a powerful Redwood family. The granddaughter of the former Alpha before he had been slain by the demon.

No, she was also a friend. One who I was not going to let die trying to protect me.

She did not deserve to get hurt because I wasn't strong enough to protect myself.

Finally, as the last vampire came at us, blood coating Skye's silver fur, as well as most of my body, I looked into the bright gold and green eyes of Skye as she gave me a tight nod, and we lunged.

The vampire grinned and shook his head. "Not today."

And then he turned, running full tilt, faster than any other vampire I'd seen—other than Valac and Sunny, the general of the vampire army and his wife. He tossed magic behind him, and black smoke filled the bubble of magic that Skye and I had found ourselves in.

I threw myself over the silver wolf, protecting her as shards of painful magic slid into my skin and threatened both of us. I knew that those icy shards of pain would dissolve quickly, as they were just there to stun, but I was stronger than Skye, and it would take longer for her to heal.

She growled low as I cradled her to my chest, covering her with my entire body before she wiggled and nipped at my ear. I pulled back and ran my hands down her fur, checking for injuries, before I slid my hands over her flank and between her ears.

"Are you okay?"

She narrowed her eyes at me. Her eyes were no longer gold with power but green with anger. She stood back and lowered her head, as if remembering I was an Alpha. I always found it odd that she could meet my gaze. I was an Alpha, and most shifters did not have the dominance to meet my gaze. Skye shouldn't either, as she wasn't a full dominant.

She was somewhere in the middle of the hierarchy, someone who could aid with the submissives and not scare them, but she wasn't a maternal either. Maternals had a set place within the Pack and cared for our young, their personal dominance of protection and caring in an interesting and needed combination.

Skye, by contrast, was somewhat odd in the structure of Packs, but it was the strength of her human self that allowed her to connect with so many of the dominants in every Pack in the Pacific Northwest.

I also had a feeling it had to do with her being the granddaughter of an Alpha and the daughter of two dominants herself. Her uncle was the current Alpha, and her cousins and aunts and uncles were all part of the hierarchy, too.

She glared at me before she began to shift her shoulders back, her body slowly going from wolf to human.

It wasn't a flash of light or a painless process. Some people could shift quickly, as if they were just breathing from one step to the next, but many took a good five minutes to break bones and tendons and twist their bodies into a new form. As our new ways of connecting to the moon goddess and Supreme Alphas settled into us, we were starting to shift far more quickly than before, but it still wasn't an easy process.

Skye was decently swift, but from the whimper that escaped from her mouth, I knew there wasn't a lack of pain from that quickness. She didn't shift as rapidly as me or her cousins.

And, by the time she knelt in her human form, her body covered in blood and sweat and grime, I could hear the footsteps of the others running towards us. Only they couldn't get through the bubble of protection, not yet, and we had to either wait for the vampire magic to subside or for one of our witches to get through. I wasn't sure when that would happen, but this did give us some privacy so Skye could finish her shift and find her balance.

I tore off my bloody shirt and tossed it to her when she looked up at me. She caught it, then stood up, naked and free, and I did my best not to look at her.

We shifters weren't supposed to notice nudity. When we shifted from one part of ourselves to the next, we didn't bring our clothes with us. It was easier to shift while we were naked, so we didn't have to tear through our clothing or end up as an awkward wolf in a shirt and pants.

Skye just tilted her head at me, and I didn't look down at the shape of her breasts, or slope of her waist, or the thatch of curls between her legs. I knew better than that, though I had seen briefly, and my mouth had watered. I couldn't help it, the urge of the hunt was still upon us, and my wolf was at the forefront, wanting her.

She might not be my mate and would never be, but Skye Anderson was beautiful. Only, I couldn't notice that just then. It wouldn't do us any good. She sighed, then slid my shirt over her shoulders.

"Are you okay?" I asked as her body was finally covered. It was easier to think that way. My wolf wanted her because it was horny, and hell, the urge of the hunt was so strong, it was probably riding her just as well. If we both hadn't been hurt, then maybe we could have let off some steam as wolves were prone to do, but now wasn't the time. And especially not with *this* wolf.

"I'm fine. Just a few claw marks. You need to get that looked after." She pointed to the bite mark on my arm, and I shrugged it off.

"The burn's almost all gone now. Wren won't even need to heal it."

"We don't know exactly what happens to bite marks. Other than sometimes they go away." She walked up towards me barefoot, her long toned legs still bare. "The last thing we need is an Alpha going down."

"I'm fine, Skye. Thank you for being out here." I frowned. "Why are you out here?"

She narrowed her eyes at me, once again meeting

my gaze. No other wolf could do that unless they were as dominant as me. The Alphas could. They were as strong if not stronger than me. But Skye shouldn't be able to. There was just something about her. The way that she folded in between magics spoke of the blood running through her veins, maybe not the dominance of her wolf.

"I was on a roam. I've been staying with Adalyn for the past week going through training."

I nodded. "I remember now. You work with knives, right?"

She nodded tightly. "My mother is the best there is at swords, and she taught me, but smaller knives I'm learning from Audrey and Adalyn. It's easier to stay with Adalyn than the newlyweds." She rolled her eyes, speaking of my Beta, Audrey, and her mate, my Tracker, Gavin.

Adalyn was a hunter for the Aspen wolves and lived alone on the far side of the den. She and Skye seemed to have become friends recently, and I wasn't sure how I felt about that.

Not because it was Skye, but because of the alliance. The Pacific Northwest Pack Alliance was something of a new construct. The Redwood Pack and the Talon Pack became friends and had nearly blended into one den over the past thirty years of mating between one another and forming bonds of friendship and trust.

The Central Pack, the fourth Pack in our little grouping of territory, was relatively new after being decimated from the Redwood War. The Centrals had brought it on themselves, and those innocents that had survived were now a new Pack with a new Alpha. Cole was my friend, and we were learning our roles as leaders of our Packs together. Cole had connections with the Talon Pack because of his sister who had mated into that den.

The Aspens, however, we were a little different. Because we had been the enemy most recently. Because of my father and the blood running through my veins. My wolf pushed at me, angry that I was even thinking about Blade, but I couldn't help it. It was in every movement and decision that we made. Because we needed to prove to the other Packs that we deserved to be within the alliance. That we weren't the enemy, or the weak ones.

Forming these relationships like Adalyn was doing with Skye was good. It was connecting us to the Redwoods, just like Audrey was connected to the Talons through the person she had turned into a cat shifter like her. Only we didn't have the same connections that the other Packs did. We were still too new in our healing and in our redemption.

If one could be redeemed from the atrocities my father had committed.

I knew that Skye being here was a form of trust from the Redwoods. I still wasn't sure how I felt about it because I didn't know exactly how long we could remain in the alliance if we were the ones the vampires constantly attacked. And if Skye had died or been hurt irrevocably in this fight? I didn't know what the Redwoods would do. Because Skye's mother was the original Redwood Pack princess, the only daughter of the former Alpha.

That meant Skye was just as much of a princess of that line as well. She might not look pampered, but I knew she was loved, cherished, and part of the Jamenson family, a tangled connection between hierarchy, dominance, strength, and blood.

And my only family was long dead, and a traitor to us all.

"Why are you looking at me like that?" Skye asked, frowning.

"I'm not looking at you like anything."

"Whatever you say." She scowled at me before looking around the weakening vampire wards. "Come on, let's get through this bubble of magic and hopefully figure out a way to make this not happen again."

"I know that your uncle's working on it, as are the rest of your family, but we are too."

Skye gave me a weird look. "I know. We have witches just like you."

"You have more witches."

She shrugged, as if unconcerned with the fact I'd mentioned our weakness—not something I tended to do. Ever. "For now. You're still regrowing your Pack. It's going to take a lot of time in order to settle yourselves. And these vampires have different magic than the witches that we know. We're all in the same boat, Chase. Remember that."

I wasn't sure I liked the fact that she was trying to settle me. It was weird. She wasn't Pack, wasn't in my hierarchy. And yet, while everybody else stepped on eggshells when it came to certain parts of my past, they also worked on protecting the Pack. They didn't worry about my own wolf. Because I was supposed to be steady, the sane one.

Only Skye seemed to want to protect me. Or maybe I was just seeing too much into it because of the vampire venom or toxin or whatever the fuck it was running through my veins.

I shook off the pain that seemed to radiate back into my system, and Skye narrowed her eyes.

"Come on, let's go get to your Healer."

We took a step forward, and I watched Steele glare at us as Dara, our harvester witch, stood next to him. She had her hands out before she sighed, sinking into my Enforcer's arms. Steele steadied her, and she shook off his touch and anyone else that was trying to help before she nodded tightly and moved past us.

"Is Dara okay?" Skye asked, her voice barely above a whisper.

I shook my head. "I don't know. She's our strongest witch, but I don't think she is taking the time she needs for herself to rest." That would be something I'd fix soon if Audrey or Hayes didn't do it first.

"I can talk to her if you want." She hopped over a fallen log, as smooth as she would have in her wolf form.

I shook my head. "It's okay. I'll do it. Or Audrey will."

Skye just shrugged. "Anything you need. We are one big alliance. I might not be Pack, but I can help."

"Thank you for your help today," I answered, my voice a little too formal.

She gave me a look, and I wanted to lean down and nip her lip, with just one fang, to tell her to stop looking at me like that. At that odd sensation, I figured it had to be because of the venom and not anything else.

"What happened?" Steele asked before Wren slid in between us, the lynx shifter frowning.

"You know I'm a Healer, but you are taking a lot of my time these days, Alpha," she joked, trying to ease her own tension. She didn't like being surrounded by so many dominants, even if she was the Healer.

As the others came out, and we told them the story

of the vampires, the teams began to do their work at cleanup, study, and investigation. The fact that we had a routine for vampire cleanup was worrying.

Wren put her hand over my arm and squeezed. My eyes crossed, and I tried not to pass out. Having me—the Alpha—fall on my knees in pain wasn't a look I needed.

I looked around my den and knew that this was only the beginning. I was not going to fall. I was not going to break. I was the Alpha. Only, something was changing. And we needed to fight. We needed to protect our den.

Skye slid past me before I could say anything, still wearing my shirt, and went to Adalyn's side, both of them talking in hushed tones.

"More vampires?" Cruz, my Heir and second in command, asked.

I nodded. "More vampires. But we got them all."

"And you were bitten," Wren whispered. "But you're going to be fine. You're all healed. In fact, your wolf has already taken care of all of it. I just did the cosmetic part."

I studied her face, wondering if she was telling the truth. She rolled her eyes but didn't meet my gaze. She was far more submissive than anyone else on my team, but she was still damn strong. My wolf would never make her back down, but her lynx did what it needed to do as well.

"They're putting their damn army right on our doorstep," Steele growled.

I nodded tightly. "They think to overpower us. To use magic that they have been hiding and cultivating for years. But we will find a way." I looked across the others and met Skye's gaze because she did not back down, did not blink, and I needed that connection. I didn't know why, but right then, I knew I needed it. I wouldn't let myself need it for long. That much I vowed.

"We are stronger. We are the Aspens. We will find out who did this and why they're here." And we *would* find out how they knew exactly where I was. Or how long they had been watching me. But that was something for another time.

"And will we be safe?" one of the maternals asked. "Can we leave the den?"

I looked at all of them, the scent of their fear acrid in my nostrils. "We are resilient. We are Pack. We will protect each other. And we will find a way to stop these attacks. We have always been fiercer than we've thought. We will not forget who we are. We will not let them win."

As my words seemed to relax most of those who had gathered, I pulled my gaze from Skye and the maternal, and I turned towards my team. "This has to stop. We have to meet with the other Alphas."

"And we have to fight. Because we are not losing our Alpha," Steele added.

I nodded slightly, but I couldn't help but wonder exactly what would happen if I was the one who was lost. What would happen to my den? Or would they be stronger because of it? I had seen the uncertainty in some gazes, and I knew I wasn't the one that they wanted to be Alpha.

I knew that they were wondering if I was Alpha enough to save them.

Because I hadn't been strong enough before. Not when I was the son of the Alpha. The son of the man who had tried to kill them all. The son of the man who had been the traitor to all shifters.

The vampires were the outside force, the ones who wanted to end us.

But, in the end, I wasn't sure if I could be the one to lead them, or if I would still be just the son who had nearly destroyed them all.

CHAPTER
TWO

Skye

"I STILL THINK I'M BETTER WITH A SWORD," MY
cousin Nico teased, and I rolled my eyes, watching him
and Adalyn train.

We stood on Redwood Pack ground, the den and
land speaking of my ancestors, family, and the power
and sacrifice that had brought our Pack to the strength
and history it now held.

Adalyn grinned, said something sharply to my
cousin, and then the two were at it, both of them using
weapons not customarily used by wolves as they trained
harder and harder.

Most wolves of my grandparents' generation swore that fighting by tooth and claw were what brought you honor. Although that might have been the case in the past, not so much anymore. During the Redwood War, when my family had fought against the demon Caym, new and unheard of enemies had walked across the land. When my family had opposed Caym, he brought in new magics and battles where wolves couldn't fight as only wolf.

My mother had picked up the sword and had learned how to fight with something other than her claws. One of my aunts had been a latent wolf for most of her life and had learned to fight with weapons as well. Not all of my aunts and uncles could shift, nor were they witches who could use magic.

Our Pack had blended over time to the point that all of us learned how to use swords, blades, guns, and other weapons to protect our Pack. I was a runner and a soldier. I wasn't dominant enough to be in the hierarchy nor blessed by the moon goddess with those powers. I also wasn't dominant enough to work directly for the Enforcer, Beta, or Alpha. I was middle of the road, but not a maternal or a submissive. It was odd because the rest of my family each had certain roles that they fulfilled, as if they'd been born to it.

I did not. I was a Redwood Pack member through and through, my wolf sang to the Redwoods, and I felt their bonds just as any other Pack member did. I went where people needed me, but never for long.

"Why do you look so sad? Are you getting your emo phase again? You already have the dark hair. If you want, we can paint your lips black and start singing depressing songs."

I flipped Nico off as Adalyn threw her hair back and laughed, looking gorgeous and radiant. From the way Nico raked his gaze down her, my cousin thought so as well.

I didn't think the two had slept together yet, but from the way they kept teasing one another, it might happen soon.

We were carnal creatures, after all, hot and ready and usually in need of someone to scratch the itch. Sex was a pleasure, but also for play and for fun. Most of the time, you could walk away from your lover with a smile on your face and a happy memory. With the idea of matings in play, hurt feelings of forever didn't usually happen. Because no matter what you were doing within that coupling at the time, there was always a chance you were still waiting for your one true happy ever after. The one person that the moon goddess and fate put in front of you to let you know that they were the one for you.

The problem was, after the moon goddess had nearly sacrificed herself to help us with the great war between the Talons and the Aspens, matings were different now. It wasn't an instantaneous recognition of mates. You didn't know that person was your potential mate just from first sight and scent. Sometimes it took longer. Sometimes it took danger, but other times it *was* that blink of an eye.

Things were far more complicated now than they had been when my parents mated.

"Did she really wear black?" Adalyn asked as she sheathed her sword in her scabbard. She pulled her hair back from her face and put it in a long ponytail on the top of her head.

"Only for a minute. Cousin Patricia over here prefers red lipstick."

"Stop calling me Patricia. You know I prefer Skye."

Nico rolled his eyes at me, but I still saw the worry there. Because it wasn't that I was upset with my name. I loved my name. I was named for the woman who had sacrificed herself to save my father.

When Caym came to the Redwood den near the end of the battle, he killed my grandparents. Grandpa Edward, the man my older brother was named after, died saving my mother, while Grandma Patricia died saving my father. In that moment, the Redwood Pack changed forever.

My Uncle Kade became Alpha, and my cousin Finn, only barely older than a toddler, had become Heir to the Pack. He'd run out into the field of battle, screaming from the pain and power of the mantle of Pack bonds that he was far too young for. That power could have gone to any other family member, or even someone not of blood. That's how it happened in other Packs now, but Finn had been the one blessed by the moon goddess—if you could call that a blessing.

My cousin was now mated, a father, and strong.

He held the power, but not the names of that sacrifice. No, that was Edward and me, and I didn't think my brother honestly cared as much as I did. He thought it was a great honor and was a dominant wolf who protected the Pack, knowing that it was his power to hold.

I just heard screaming. Though I didn't know why. It wasn't like I had been alive when that happened. But I could still hear my mother's screams in my sleep.

I had to wonder what the moon goddess had blessed me with if nothing but a name and a legacy that I wasn't sure I could live up to.

"Are you coming to the Aspen den tomorrow to train with Audrey?" Adalyn asked as she sat down on the rock next to me.

I looked over at my new friend and smiled. Adalyn was a tall warrior. She had reddish-brown hair and green eyes and looked like she could kill a man with just her pinky. Considering she was a hunter for the Aspens, that could be something she actually did.

"I plan on it. Unless one of the uncles or cousins needs me for something else."

Nico was looking down at his phone, scrolling at something as he frowned. "No, you're free to train with them. They like us going over there."

He winked, and I shook my head. "Why do I feel that you're up to something, cousin of mine?"

"Because I'm usually up to something. But come on, there's how many of us cousins? I think the parents like it when we get out, but know we are safer within den wards."

"I know that Chase likes me within the wards, too," Adalyn said, re-tying her shoe. "But he also likes all of the other Pack members coming in and out of the den. At least, those he trusts fully. It shows a level of trust on both sides to have a near-open door with so many of our allies. It's good to have new blood within the den wards. Especially with so many new actual full-blooded Pack members now. It makes it feel like home again."

There were many things I could say to that, at the pain in Adalyn's words. Because I knew she had been through hell when she was with the Aspens underneath the "tutelage" of the former Alpha. I hadn't known Blade, hadn't fought him in battle alongside some of the Redwoods and the Talons. My job at the time had been to be with the Redwoods. To protect the pups on den land, in case some of the Aspens attacked our den. At the time, they had only attacked the Talons, but I'd lost one of my cousins in the battle.

I could practically feel the pain of Nico's wolf, and I knew he was remembering the same things I was. We had fought in many battles over the past few years against humans, demons, and fellow wolves. We had lost friends, Packmates, and those close to us. It was during the final battle with the humans in which we'd gained our independence and taken down the tyrannical politician and his army that had wanted to use us for their own gain, that we'd lost our cousin Blake.

Somehow within my family, no matter how large we were, with my numerous aunts and uncles and even more cousins, we hadn't lost anyone since my grandparents.

But Blake, my cousin twice over, had died. My mother was sister to Blake's father, and my father was brother to Blake's mother. Brothers and sisters marrying across Pack lines, with the mating full force to bring us stronger.

I still didn't think my Uncle North and Aunt Lexi were fully healed from burying their son. Not that I expected them to be. We all mourned Blake, and I knew that Adalyn also mourned those she'd lost within her den. I didn't know everything that happened when the

Aspens had been on the wrong side of history, but I knew they were coming back from it. Just like we were trying to come back from our loss.

"You know, I bet you Chase likes coming over to the den for other things, too," Adalyn teased, and I shot her a look as Nico came forward, phone long forgotten, and eyes widened.

"Okay, what did I miss?"

"Nothing," I snapped.

"Well, you know they were out in the moonlight when the vampires attacked, then there they were, fighting side by side, and suddenly they come out of the magical darkness with her just wearing his shirt, and my Alpha wearing nothing but pants and bloody shoes."

"Adalyn," I snapped, even as my wolf pushed at me, just wanting to play along.

Only, one did not play along with the Alpha of the Pack. I was not an Alpha's mate, nor someone that should play with an Alpha. My cousin, Brie, was a submissive wolf and yet an Alpha's mate. She was the highest-ranking wolf alongside her mate within the Talons and led with compassion, not outer strength. Fate had had a funny trick to that, but I was not my cousin. I was so far in the middle of the hierarchy that my wolf didn't know what she was doing. It did not make sense for me to even joke about being with the Alpha of the Aspens.

"What were you doing in the woods, cousin?" Nico teased, his wolf in his gaze.

"I was running on patrol and coming towards the den to speak with Adalyn. You know that. I already gave my report to Uncle Kade."

Nico narrowed his gaze. "There was no mention of you wearing the Alpha's shirt."

"Because I was in wolf form, and when I shifted back to make sure the vampire bite on his arm was fine, I was naked. He handed over his shirt so I wouldn't be."

Adalyn grinned, looking unrepentant. "Seems to me wolves shouldn't care that they're naked."

I narrowed my gaze between them, knowing that they were having fun ganging up on me. "Since we had been in the middle of a fight, I appreciated the clothing. I don't like being bare in front of another person while they're clothed, especially with both of us covered in blood. I'm sorry that I'm not as dominant as you, Adalyn," I snarled, and then regretted the words as soon as I said them.

Adalyn's gaze widened, her wolf at the forefront. "I'm so sorry. I didn't know that would hurt you. Are you okay?"

I lowered my gaze, not because I had to, but because it was what my wolf was supposed to do.

That was the problem with my wolf. She didn't always do what she needed to. I had never been one to lower my gaze from someone more dominant. It wasn't that I wasn't submissive, because I was far more submissive than Adalyn and Nico.

Nico's strength was in his speed. Because he was part witch, his magical talent and affinity towards earth let him use the earth magic itself to sprint. He had power from magic and his wolf. Adalyn was strong, so strong that I was shocked that she wasn't part of the actual hierarchy and blessed by the goddess. I thought she should have been the Enforcer, but I didn't know much about the ongoing relations of the Aspen Pack.

My wolf, however, did not cower to either one of them. It should have. It didn't matter that they were my friends and family. My wolf should have lowered her gaze. But I didn't need to. It didn't matter that I knew I was more submissive than them. It didn't matter that I didn't have the strength and power that they did.

My wolf was just weird.

Broken.

And that was my secret.

I waved them off, embarrassed that I had even lashed out as I had. They'd been teasing and didn't deserve my attitude. "It's fine. I didn't mean it like that. I was snarking because I don't like you insinuating that I have any thirst for the Alpha."

"Oh, cousin, I don't believe Adalyn mentioned

thirst." Nico winked as he said it, and I knew he was trying to cut the tension, but I cringed.

"There is no thirst."

Adalyn buffed her nails on her shirt. "I don't know. Chase is quite tasty."

My eyebrows shot up. "You and Chase?" I asked, aghast.

Adalyn just threw her head back and laughed, looking gorgeous as ever. I saw Nico narrow his eyes, and now I wondered exactly what was going on with these two, or if I was just seeing things because I needed to.

"Nothing has ever happened between Chase and me. I'm not even sure Chase knows how to relax enough to let his wolf play like that. He's far too busy being the perfect Alpha."

"Okay, now I'm curious." I leaned forward. "What's wrong, Adalyn?"

She gave me a soft smile. "That's not my story to tell, and I probably said too much. But Chase is good. He's just focused on our Pack, as we all should be. The fact that Audrey found her mate Gavin as she did after everything that happened is a blessing. The mating bond with our Beta at so high in the hierarchy brings us strength, just like you know that mating brings strength to your Pack."

"We do," I said at the same time as Nico.

"Although we don't have as many matings in our new generation of wolves as we do with the old guard," he added.

That was true. Unlike with the Talons, and even the Aspens, our new generation of hierarchy hadn't come into power because of death. My aunt and uncles had held the mantles of Omega, Healer, and Enforcer for over a century. Because they had, when the next generation had come into power, the moon goddess shared responsibilities between the two. While we technically only had one of each title now, our uncles and Aunt Hannah all helped in some way. They still retained some of their power, making us stronger than most Packs even now.

We hadn't had to lose our family in order to bring power to the new generation. That was so unlike most Packs these days. It brought hope to most of us.

But that also meant that only our cousin, the Enforcer, Gina was mated. The rest of us were all unmated, though the older generation balanced us with their matings.

In the end, we were stronger for it, and most wolves didn't find their mates in their twenties and thirties. So none of us were worried that we hadn't found our mates. Sometimes it took centuries to find the person—or people in some cases—that were perfect for you.

"So you're not out there looking for a mate then?"

Nico teased, and Adalyn rolled her eyes before picking up her sword again.

"Okay, Skye, it's time for you to show me your sword skills."

"I have a penis joke in that, but I'm just not in the mood with my cousin around," Nico teased.

Adalyn's gaze went gold, her wolf at the forefront. "Maybe later, wolf."

I cringed but let the two flirt before I pulled out my sword and got ready.

"You know my mother taught me. You better beware."

"Oh, I know Cailin taught you. I want her to teach me, as well."

I narrowed my gaze. "Excuse me? No. I'm going to be the one that teaches you. You don't need my mother."

"Them's fighting words," Nico called out from the outside of the training ring.

"Damn straight," I teased.

"Well then. You'll teach me the sword, Audrey will teach us both knives, and I guess I'll have to find something to teach you," Adalyn added.

"I can think of something!" Nico called out.

I quickly flipped him off, and as he laughed, Adalyn and I began to move. It was sword against sword, blade against blade. Even as sweat began to slick down my back, I kept moving, my feet in perfect harmony. It was like dancing to me, moving with the blade as if I'd been doing it for years. And I had been. Most of my siblings and cousins had learned other weapons, a sword being something of an ancient practice. But my mother had loved it, as her mother had taught her. So she taught me.

I was my mother's daughter, my mother's mother's daughter. I was of the earth, of wolves, and I was of magic.

And as the clash of steel rang out into the air and my wolf ran to the forefront, I knew I would find my purpose one day.

But for now, I would move with the grace I was born with.

And I would fight.

Even if I wasn't sure who I was fighting for.

CHAPTER
THREE

Chase

I RAN MY HAND THROUGH MY HAIR AND PACED MY bedroom, willing my wolf to calm down. I was the Alpha, after all. I had to show control of my wolf and the power in my veins.

It wasn't that my wolf wanted to take over and rampage the den as a rogue would. It was more that I needed to *run* again. But that was how I had gotten in trouble in the first place. How we had even found the nest of vampires recently. I needed time in the wild. I needed to feel the wind on my face and in my fur. And I needed to pretend that I was okay.

No longer did I want to remember the touch of steel and silver along my body as I hunched in a too-small cage, trying to find my way out. I could no longer be that person. I had to be stronger than that.

My wolf pawed at me, finally calming down.

"We'll go on a run soon. Though probably with Steele or Cruz."

My wolf huffed, mollified, and I shook my head.

Not everybody had the same connections to their wolves that I did. Shifters had been born unto the world by the moon goddess herself. Long ago, when she'd come upon a hunter killing a wolf for gain and not food, she'd bound their souls to save the wolf and teach the human about life. From there, the shifters were born, two souls within one body, a delicate balance of strength and heart.

I knew some Packs could even talk to their wolves, as if the soul that shared their body spoke to them in full sentences.

I didn't have that, but when I had been locked alone in a cage thanks to my father's attentions, my wolf had been my only friend—the only one who could keep me safe and keep me company for all of those years.

Others had come into the cages beside me, some had never left. Audrey had been there, of course, but she had been the one to escape. The one who had come back to save us all.

I hadn't been so lucky, but I'd had my wolf to speak to. And though he didn't answer back in words, I could still feel the bond between us, soul to soul, shifter to human to animal.

My wolf had been my best friend even when I hadn't been allowed to shift.

He was the one that I leaned on when I'd had no one else.

There was a knock on the door, and then Steele walked in as if he owned the place.

I narrowed my eyes at my Enforcer, who just rolled his. His hair was dark, his eyes bright blue, though the ring of gold around the iris told me that his wolf was at the forefront.

"Problem?"

Steele shook his head. "No, other than the fact that we're going to be late to the meeting with the Alphas."

"Are we sure that having a meeting with all of us in one place is a good idea?" I asked.

"They're not going to get through our wards, damn it," Steele growled.

I nodded. "I know they won't because you know what you're doing, Steele. You're a good wolf. A good Enforcer. I trust you." I put my hand on the back of Steele's neck, and I could feel the tension ease out of the other man as he lowered his head, a breath wheezing from his lungs.

"I don't like the fact that we don't have some strong enough witches to keep our wards going."

"It used to be that the power of our wolves was what kept it strong once the witches set the wards. But I suppose things changed after the wards fell during the last war."

"Dara's doing her best. But we don't have anyone else."

"Lily?" I asked, mentioning the earth witch who was weak in power but strong in determination.

"She's trying, but it's not enough. We need more witches in the den, just like we're adding more wolves to our fold. Is there a way we can do that?"

"Perhaps a job fair," I said as I lowered my hand, and Steele's eyes hardened.

"Really?"

"I don't know. Putting our shingle out for the wolves worked, for those lone wolves or wolves that were a little out of the hierarchy like Gavin was in the Thames Pack. Perhaps we can do that for the witches." I let out a breath. "Witches that are having trouble in the coven. Or do not have a coven."

"We need to get them mated into the den. That would be the best way."

I smiled at that. I couldn't help it. "Yes. You get right on that. You go find your fated mate after all of these years and make sure she's a witch."

Steele narrowed his eyes at me. "I was talking about you. You're the Alpha. Having the Beta mated is great and all for the den, but what about you?"

"Like I said. It's just easy to find that fated mate. I could pick her up at the grocery store, right? Right next to that carton of milk."

"Perhaps if you actually got out and dated once in a while, you could find that mate of yours."

I shook my head as the two of us made our way over to the council chambers, where we were meeting the other Alphas. "Yes. Because I can see you letting me leave the damn den these days. Just so I can go on a date."

"You keep going on these runs alone to let off steam. Maybe you should do that in another way, and that would help things."

We passed by a group of maternals, and I nodded at them, smiling. They waved back, going back to their conversation.

"Are you telling me that I need to get laid for the good of the den?"

"I'm sure our Healer and Omega will be the ones to tell you that. I'm just the one that knows when there are outside forces coming at us. Perhaps the Heir and the Beta can help as well."

"Good to know you're thinking about me." I hadn't corrected him on my reason for needing to run. Nobody needed to know those reasons. I needed to be a strong Alpha, not weak.

They needed to know I was strong.

"Who else is going to be here?" I asked, though I knew most of the answers.

"Kade from the Redwoods, Gideon from the Talons, and Cole from the Centrals as usual. The other Alphas will be on the screens, though I'm not sure all of them will get in on this one."

I nearly tripped over my feet as we turned the corner. "They're not going to join us for an Alpha Pack conclave?" I asked, incredulously.

"I have a feeling that some of the Alphas might think that it is our fault that the vampires are attacking the Pacific Northwest. Not that they want vampires to attack them, but some others not allied as closely might believe we brought this onto ourselves by somehow causing it."

I mulled that over, knowing that some of the conflicts this area had gone through in the past were of our own making, but not all of them. While I didn't want the rest of the world to deal with this either, I wasn't happy thinking that others once again thought the Aspen Pack was doing harm to itself. "Riaz from the Starlights will be there, right?"

"As far as I know. Plus, he had his own issues that are remarkably similar to this." Steele spoke of the rogue situation the Starlight Pack had been forced to deal with down in Texas that had twisted the narrative of a rogue wolf, leaving more questions than answers.

"Meaning it's not just us."

"We all knew that before. But you know the stigma of this area."

We were the first wolves to be forced out into the public. Therefore, we had thrown the secrecy of our race into the world for everyone else to see. Not everybody had a say in the matter. Hell, *nobody* had a damn choice in the matter. We might've been able to stay secret from the humans for longer than most, but that was because we were good at keeping secrets because of the other members of our Pack, such as bear and cat shifters. We still kept those secrets, so nobody knew they existed. I knew some Packs were still closeted. Even after all these years, they were able to keep who they were away from the rest of the world. Only I didn't think that was going to last much longer.

The President of United States was connected to a Pack of his own through his daughter's mating with a wolf. And we had other members joining the government as they always had. No longer to keep our secrets, but to keep our safety. The government had to know that those Packs existed. Even if the public didn't. Soon there would be no more time for anyone to hide. And with the threat of the vampires on the rise, I didn't think hiding was a good option anymore.

"We'll talk about that later," I said, as we walked inside, and the other Alphas turned to me as one.

Because we did not age like humans, we all looked around the same age, in our early thirties, maybe Kade looked a little older with his life experience.

But two wolves in this room were easily over a century, if not more. Cole and I were the young ones, although I still had a good twenty years on the young pup.

Cole had become an Alpha before me, but only by a few months, maybe a year. We were on the same track, finding out who we were as leaders, Alphas, and in Packs that were born from the shambles and flames of disaster and betrayal.

There were other people in the room, of course, wolves in the hierarchy, a few witches, but everyone was of one of the four Packs. On the screens were Allister and Riaz, as well as a few other Alphas that we were friendly with. There were a few noticeable people missing, but I had to hope that we'd find a way to mend those fences later.

"So, a vampire on the doorstep, was it?" Gideon asked, brow raised, and I snorted.

"Yes. One with pointy, pointy teeth."

"Did the bite heal?" Kade asked, his gaze going to my arm.

I hadn't mentioned that I had been bitten, so when the others looked at Kade, he shrugged.

"Skye mentioned it."

I turned to the woman in the corner, that familiar scent hitting my nostrils. I had known she was in the room, just as I knew everyone who was in the room. My wolf had spotted each person, even if I couldn't see them directly. I knew Steele had done much of the same.

Skye met my gaze in that odd way of hers and shrugged. "Sorry. Didn't know it was a secret."

Steele growled, and I snorted.

"Not a secret. But thank you. For saving me."

The other Alphas and wolves looked on with interest as Skye lowered her gaze. "You could've saved yourself. I just happened to be there."

"Yes, it's good that you were there," Cole said as he hugged Skye close. She grinned up at him, and I hadn't realized that the two were friends. Or perhaps I should have. She had grown up alongside some of Cole's former Pack members.

"I am glad that I was there when I was because then I could see the magic that these guys were throwing out."

"And that's why we're here," Gideon put in as he took a seat. Since he had, everyone else relaxed marginally and we all sat down as well. That was the strength of Gideon. We were all nearly equal in dominance. Deciding who was going to sit first and show inherent weakness or even strength because they were the ones able to sit first was a choice. It was always a chess match when you had so many dominant personalities and wolves in a room at the same time. But Gideon and Kade had played at this game often enough, that even though they were friends, family even, they knew how to interact and not rile up their wolves. It allowed Cole and me to follow suit without feeling any less dominant than they were.

My wolf was content and partially interested in the woman in the corner. Not that I was going to let him be. Just because I found her attractive didn't mean I had time for that, no matter what Steele wanted me to do.

"I don't like the fact that they're getting so close, and they have this magic that we don't seem to have," Cole said after a moment, breaking the tension.

I nodded tightly. "Agreed. They're using a dark magic that we don't have access to." I looked at the others for confirmation, and even those on the screens above us nodded.

"We have some of the strongest witches out there, and we don't even know."

"What does the coven think?" I asked.

Kade's jaw tightened, and I sensed something was wrong there.

"The coven as we know it is no more."

That dropped like an anvil, and we all turned to him.

"What?"

"The witches of our Pack have never been full coven because they were Pack. And alliances have always been one or the other. But the coven leaders from before, the ones who had done their best to come out of the ashes of war after war, have now been overtaken by newer witches."

"What does that mean?"

"They're witches who only want those of pure blood. No connections to the Packs, or those with powers that have been mutated by any others."

I gaped at Gideon, then looked over at Cole. "Did you know any of this?"

"It's the first time I'm hearing of it," he growled.

Both of the other Alphas raised their palms, a gesture to ward off my anger apparently. Their wolves were in their gazes and I let out a deep breath, controlling my own.

"We just heard about it right before we got here. That means when we meet with the full council, we'll have two new members to meet since the coven is making up their own rules right now."

The council was a group of non-Alphas from each Pack, as well as members from the coven and other magical communities that might not be part of a bigger structure. It's how we protected ourselves, and it was the beginning of our alliance. The Alphas came to some council meetings. Cole and I tended to go to all of them since we were still showing our power and learning. Kade and Gideon came when needed and tried to rely on their stronger Pack structure to get the information. One day, if we healed enough and grew to where we needed to be, Cole and I would function in the same way.

"So, these young witches, they are kicking out anybody that isn't perfect?" I asked.

"Yes. And I know you have Dara within your den," Kade put in.

I stiffened. "Yes?"

"Keep her safe. They only want elemental witches in power. And when she was hidden as a weak witch, even though I'm not sure she ever was, the coven didn't care. But now that the stories of her saving the den are out? Beware."

I growled, my wolf at the forefront. "I'll be damned if anyone touches my Pack. Dara is ours."

"Damn straight," Gideon growled.

"So what we're saying is," Cole interrupted, "the coven is infighting, our witches are scattered, and we don't have the magical powers within our Packs in order to fight the vampires."

I nodded in agreement, my wolf pushing at me. Wanting to claw anything just then. "In other words, we're fucked."

"Succinct, I like it," Riaz said with a growl.

"We have our own coven issues here; something's going on in the magical communities, and I have a feeling it has to do with those magics that these vampires are using," Allister put in.

I nodded as we all began to talk, trying to come up with a plan to get more magical powers to protect ourselves. We had always had a difficult relationship with witches, even when we had been hidden from them. We had never been on the outs, except for possibly a few skirmishes over time. But things were changing.

And with the vampires coming at us and using magic that was previously unheard of, I was worried. Damn worried.

And, as the meeting came to an end, all of us agreed to do our best to put out that shingle for witches and wanting to protect those that the coven might not protect anymore. I found myself standing alone outside of the Aspen council building as the others left, and that familiar scent hit my nose.

"Are you okay?" Skye asked, and I turned to her, my brow raised.

"You should be asking your uncle that."

"Because he's my Alpha? Or because he sounded even growlier than you did after that meeting?"

My lips twitched despite myself, and I shook my head. "Maybe a little bit of both."

She was meeting my gaze again, and my wolf didn't back down. Didn't push at her. It was just intrigued because he didn't understand how she could do that.

"We'll figure it out because we're together. All of us."

"I wish I had your optimism, Skye."

"You're the Alpha. You don't get to be optimistic. You're realistic, as you protect us all."

I tilted my head, studying her. "That's one way to look at it."

"It's the only way as far as I'm concerned. But you've got this, Chase. We'll find the magical means in order to protect the wards. We can do this."

The wind rustled and her hair blew in front of her face a bit. Without thinking, I pushed a strand behind her ear, and I heard the swift intake of her breath.

"Alpha," she whispered.

"Skye."

We stood there, my fingers gently brushing her skin, before a wolf howled, just in fun and joyous for their run, and the moment was broken. Skye took a step back and cleared her throat. "I need to go back with my uncle. I've lingered too long."

I swallowed hard, ignoring my wolf—and my cock pressing against my jeans.

"Thank you, Skye."

"For what?" she asked, her face scrunched.

"For reminding me exactly what an Alpha is."

"I don't know if I did that. Sometimes I feel like I'm just figuring it out."

And with that, she turned on her heel, and I swallowed hard, wondering exactly what the hell had just happened.

CHAPTER
FOUR

Skye

"Do you feel like we were forced into this position because nobody else wanted the role?" Nico asked from my side, and I turned to my cousin, raising a brow.

"Say it louder for the people in the back, why don't you?" I asked, even though I felt the same way.

Nico and I, along with a few other soldiers and members from other Packs, were on bodyguard duty for the day.

The council was meeting to try to put together a plan against the magic the vampires used. It was a real threat. Yet, as Nico and I stood and listened to others we didn't know very well bicker, I didn't think that much would get done today. Not with the way the witches were smirking at one another.

"I miss Amelia and Diana."

My wolf mourned, howling deep inside at the mention of the two women. They had been the coven representatives on the council, and through time, war, and life, they were gone to us. The coven was in a state of flux, jockeying for power, and the council members rotated.

I didn't know the current council members. I didn't even know their names. I would, after this, as it would be my job to keep our two council members safe. And that meant knowing your enemy.

It was odd to think that the coven again *could* be our enemy.

The coven was a collection of witches that governed witch society. Yet, not everybody was part of that coven. Because it was a political race. Everybody wanted power, to tell people how to use their magic, but the construct of that magic wasn't like a den. It wasn't a Pack, with an Alpha and a Beta and the moon goddess protecting them. Every witch was individual, how they came into their power, how they used their power, and the coven was supposed to be there to protect them. To teach those younger and coming into their magics. And yet, that wasn't what was happening.

Now it was sanctioning and deciding who was allowed to use their powers. Only, that didn't make much sense to me because nobody could control that type of power. At least as far as I knew. I wasn't sure what the coven was up to, and they weren't keen on letting us into the discussions, at least not a lowly soldier like me.

"Do you think anything's going to be accomplished today?" Nico asked, and I shook my head.

"I don't know. It's a little worrying."

Farah, our cousin Gina, and our aunt Lexi were our charges for the day. Other members of the Pack could normally come and go, but right now it was a closed council, with three members from each of the four local Packs, four coven members, as well as our Supreme Alphas—Max and Cheyenne.

Over the past few years, the people had changed as duties needed to be replaced or put elsewhere. Some of the originals were still there, even if they might have titles and positions in other parts of the Pack. They were still here as council members, as voices who weren't Alphas but were there to hear the needs of the Packs as a whole. Because sometimes Alpha to Alpha or even Beta to Beta, things slid through the cracks. The needs of friendship and connections from people not so high up in the hierarchy deserved attention, too.

Farah was a wolf and a friend. She had been part of the original Redwood Pack council structure. My cousin Gina was our Enforcer. She, like Steele of the Aspens, protected the den. Our uncle Adam had been the original Enforcer of the Redwood Pack and still held some of the power, and continued working together with Gina to make the Pack stronger than ever.

I liked that she was a council member. Because she was always alert, always protective, but she was also mated to a former Talon Pack member. The first connection that had brought our Packs to peace and full friendship.

Lexi was the newer member of the rotating council members. I knew she mourned her son—our cousin— Blake. She stood with such grace and strength that it broke me sometimes to think she was screaming inside. A mother who lost her son far too young, in a war that shouldn't have happened, was what made her good to have on the council.

It also meant that I kept a close watch on her. I didn't want anyone to think that she was weak for still mourning. Nor did I want her to have too much on her shoulders when she was already carrying so much herself.

On the Talon side, there were the usual members,

including Leah, a water witch who was a Talon Pack member, separate from the coven.

Considering my Pack also included witches who had been mated in or born into it, I understood that not every witch was part of the coven because you couldn't divide your loyalties that way. But, from the way that the new coven leader was glaring at Leah, Henrick didn't agree.

That made me look towards the four coven members who had come to take their places.

Henrick had taken control of the coven, and I didn't know exactly how. Perhaps the Alphas did, but, from the way that Chase and Cole—both attending as guests of the council as they were there as newer Alphas—were glaring at the man, they didn't like him much.

Anastasia was the coven's second in command and was also by his side. They were adjunct council members and, like Cole and Chase, didn't need to come every time there was a full meeting. But since the two were relatively new to their positions, they showed up often.

Rose and Stanley were both new council members from the coven. I didn't know them or what they repre-sented. Nor did I know their magic, but I had a feeling all four had to be elementals—witches who used fire, earth, water, or air magic. They didn't like any magic that was outside the norm. My friend Dara, a harvester death witch, wasn't one that they would ever accept. That meant I would do all in my power to keep her safe, just like I would for my Pack.

I met Chase's gaze for a minute, and he raised a brow before going back to what Henrick was saying. I was listening, keeping my ear open for the drawl of conversation, but I wasn't paying attention. I'd be able to recall what they were saying later and go through it, but for now, my job was to keep the peace and to keep the Redwoods safe.

"We need to focus on the magics that these vampires are using," Lexi put in, for what felt like the third time.

Leah nodded. "Agreed. We're working together to come up with what dark magics they're using to keep us out of their personal wards. There's also the dark magic to lure others to them when we're not watching. But I can't figure out what it is. What about you?" Leah asked the coven side of the table, but Henrick just gave a placid smile as if he were humoring everyone by being there.

"Those magics are not of the coven nor a witch power. These *vampires*, as you call them, must be of demon nature." He grinned over at the Redwood side of the table. "And you would know all about the demons, wouldn't you?" Then he raised a finger. "No, that was the Centrals that brought the demon into our realm, wasn't it?" he asked.

In its former iteration, the Central Pack had brought the demon Caym into our world. The former sadistic Alpha had killed others to make it happen, and many of my aunts and uncles had been hurt, and I had lost my grandparents because of that demon.

But it wasn't the Centrals that sat on the other side of the table. These Centrals were the children of the elders that had been rescued and hidden away. They weren't tainted by greed and death.

But, from the way that Henrick was smiling like a cat who had nibbled on the canary, he didn't agree.

"You're right. The original Central Pack did bring forth the demon." Cole gave a tight-lipped smile. "And, when those Centrals died, it was the Redwood and Talon Packs that sent that demon back."

Henrick waved his hand as if his words hadn't been a landmine. "And yet something must have stayed. Because now we have vampires, with this *magic* as you like to call it, and yet what does that mean? Who's exactly at fault here?"

"We are not looking for fault," Chase snarled. I met his gaze, hoping he would calm down. These witches didn't like confrontation unless they were the ones dishing out. That much I could tell. And I knew Chase was on edge, and I also knew that he probably wasn't sleeping. He was starting to get circles under his eyes, the weight of the responsibility of an Alpha weighing on him. And I understood it, but we couldn't give Henrick the satisfaction of knowing that he was getting under our skin. Even if I wanted to slap the grin off the witch's face.

"If you don't want to call it magic, and you want to use sorcery, use whatever words you'd like, but these nests of vampires—beings with fangs who like to suck blood, beings who call themselves vampires—are here. They are attacking us. And not just the Aspens. And not just in the Pacific Northwest. More sightings are being reported around the country as we speak. But, if the leaders are here thanks to the demons, we are on the front lines, and we need to find a way to protect our Packs and protect our people. You are the ones with magic. What are you doing to aid in this battle?"

I wanted to stand up and clap, but I leaned against the wall, doing my best to look nonchalant, even as I was ready to tear out the throat of anyone who came at us. I might not be the most dominant person in the room, in fact, I was probably lower on the scale than most here, but I could still fight. And I had my blades. I would do what needed to be done. I just really hoped I wouldn't have to.

Anastasia cleared her throat, a little cough that grated on my nerves. "As you can tell, we are new in our positions and just coming to terms with exactly what magic our people have. We are doing our best to find out what *sorcery* these beings are using. I'm not quite sure what else you expect us to do." Her voice was breathy and so calm it made me want to strangle her.

If this was the best of the new coven, I wasn't impressed.

Gina, who was a witch and a wolf, narrowed her eyes, and I hoped that my cousin wouldn't go over and slap the woman. I wouldn't mind it, but they weren't wolves, and they said that we had to abide by *their* rules.

Max and Cheyenne, the Supreme Alphas, the two that the moon goddess had blessed with the power to protect the wolves of the world, looked at each other, then cleared their throats.

"I think what we need to do is combine our forces," Cheyenne said.

Cheyenne had been born human and was new into her powers as a wolf and Alpha, and I wasn't sure how she was able to do all of this, but I trusted her. My wolf trusted her completely, implicitly. And that meant the human part of me did, too.

Max was far older and had been born a wolf. But he wasn't used to this power, that much I could tell, yet he walked into his strength as if he had been made for it.

He lost his arm in the battle that Lexi's son had perished in. We were all still hurting from the wars we had fought, but there was no going back, no trying to calm this because we were in a fight for our lives, even if the witches didn't think it.

"I don't know what magic you expect us to do," Henrick said. "Do you want us to succumb to the dark magics that they are using? To taint our souls and our powers' pureness to combat this magic that you say exists? No, I don't believe so."

"So you're just going to not help?" Chase asked incredulously. I was with him on that, and my wolf pushed at me, angry.

"I don't know what you expect us to do," Anastasia added. "We don't have their magic. It doesn't feel like witch magic. Perhaps you should find a vampire and ask him."

My mouth dropped, as did some of the others, as we stared at the four witches who didn't seem to care at all that our safety and lives were threatened.

"So, that's it? We just pretend that everything's okay while you guys offer no help at all?" Cole asked as he let out a soft laugh. "Because, even if you can't protect us against the vampires, what about the wards?"

"What do the wards have anything to do with us?" Henrick asked as he picked a piece of lint off his sleeve.

Chase let out a sigh as the others shifted in their seats.

"The witches have always helped with the wards of

our dens," Max said softly, calmly. "Are you reneging on your promises of your forefathers?" he asked.

"Promises were made centuries ago. But they were never treaties. You have witches of your own, those not of coven and not of pureness. Use them. We need to protect ourselves. We said that we do not have the magic of these vampires, and we don't. Meaning we will not fight them until we know what we can do against them. For now, use what you have. You have always said you were the strongest. Use that strength."

And with that, the four stood up, ready to go. Everybody burst out talking at once, and I had a feeling that if this didn't change now, we would lose the coven forever. We needed them. All of us needed to be together against this foe, and yet the coven was just going to walk away?

An explosion rang out before anyone could say anything. I moved, going over to Lexi's side to protect her. She snarled at me, her wolf in her gaze.

"Out of the building, it's coming down around us."

I nodded tightly as I helped move the others through the doorway.

The council meeting area was in the neutral zone, as we called it. Not on any Pack land, but on a strip owned by everyone equally.

While it had wards, it didn't have wards of Pack, but wards of friendship and trust.

Wards that required the witches.

The witches that were no longer aiding.

"What is this?" Henrick asked, his words as pompous as ever.

"This is who we've been fighting," Chase snarled as he came to my side. I didn't even think he realized he had done it. But as the small nest of vampires came at us, the smell of smoke in the air as whatever magical bomb they had used began to disperse, we stood as we had in the forest, ready to fight together. Everyone had come together, even the submissives and maternals who were part of the council. We could all fight, and it wasn't as if we could run away at this point.

"There's only eleven of them, from what I can tell," Chase growled, and the others around us nodded.

"Protect us," Henrick snarled. "We don't have this type of magic to fight whatever these are. You brought these forth. You take them out."

I glared at the witch, knowing that he would be of no help. I was here as bodyguard, and that's what I would do. The first vampire came at us, reaching his hand toward us, I pushed Chase down, knowing that it was my job to protect him.

The inky black magic slapped into my arm and shoulder, and I hit the ground cursing.

The vampire had shot that spell or whatever it was called directly at Chase, and I wouldn't let him get hurt. My job was to protect the Alphas, which I would do.

But the pain lashing my body intensified as the black dust or whatever it was seeped into my skin, burning me from the inside out. I screamed as the other wolves went and killed the vampires quickly, as if they were only there to be a show. It wasn't even a full force, just weaklings that were only half crazed, the only one with any sense of knowledge in its gaze the one that had tried to kill Chase.

And then Chase was over me as I was on the ground convulsing, heat and fiery pain slicing through me.

"You little idiot," he barked as he ripped the top of my shirt down and looked down at the wound.

"How bad is it?" I tried to gasp out, my teeth chattering.

"We need a witch!" he called out, and then Leah was there, kneeling beside me.

"I'll see what I can do. The other wolves are taking down the vampires."

"Help her," Chase snapped, but Leah didn't back down or even look worried.

"I'll get her. We've got this. It's just on the surface."

"It feels a little deeper," I rasped, blood slowly beginning to seep out of my mouth.

It felt as if I were being stabbed a thousand times over and over again in my shoulder, but then Leah's water magic was seeping like a balm over my arm. Chase was holding me, keeping me down as I began to thrash, the coolness of her water magic feeling as if it were putting out the flames in my body. Only there was no steam. It felt as if I was burning from the inside out, but from the outside nobody could tell. It was just a burn mark along my shoulder and upper arm and a small trickle of blood from my lip where I bit down.

"You're going to be okay," Leah whispered, and I hoped she was right.

The other wolves were all around us, Nico cursing as he paced around me as if to rip out the throat of anyone who came near.

Lexi's eyes were wide, haunted, and I didn't want her to see this. *I couldn't let her see this.* Only I couldn't open my mouth to speak.

It was Chase who held me. Not my Alpha, not my Pack, but the man I had protected, the man I should always protect. He held me close as Leah used her magic to heal me, and the other witches stood by and did nothing.

I would always remember this.

Always.

And from the look in Chase's gaze, so would he.

"You're okay. We got it out." Leah wiped the back of her hand over her forehead. "Thank the goddess."

That made me snort, even as I hurt. "Good to know our magic works on it."

Leah smiled softly, even as exhaustion settled over her face. "You're right. I don't know what that was."

"What that was, was you pushing me down when I should have been the one to take that," Chase snapped above me. I looked up at him.

"It would've hit you directly in the chest, over your heart. I wasn't going to let an Alpha get hurt."

"We'll talk about this later," Chase whispered.

The others looked away, as if not wanting to be part of this. I just sighed and knew that he wouldn't be the only one yelling at me. No, Nico would growl, as would probably my Alpha and my father.

Chase could have been hurt, far beyond me. I had twisted right at the right moment so I didn't get it full in the face or the chest.

That vampire had been coming for Chase. Just like he had before. And I wasn't going to let Chase get hurt.

Even if he hated me for it.

And even if it felt like I had been one step closer to dying than I had ever planned.

CHAPTER
FIVE

Chase

IN THE DAYS SINCE THE ATTACK ON THE COUNCIL meeting, things were a whirlwind. I wasn't sure if the coven would join us again or if they would fully break off from the council completely. I didn't have a say on what they did, but I could protect my people in any way possible. It didn't make it any easier.

If we didn't find a way to combine our magic as Packs without the coven, I wasn't sure what we would be able to do when the vampire nests increased in ferocity.

It worried me because I didn't have an answer. And the Pack was relying on me.

"You're growling to yourself again," Audrey said from my side as she sipped her wine. I looked over at my second in command, my Beta, and scowled.

"I'm not doing anything."

"You're overthinking and stressing out when we're supposed to have five minutes to ourselves tonight. Just five minutes to breathe and to focus on who we are. And yet, you are in your own head, probably thinking about things that you can't fix right away on your own."

I glared at Audrey, who just smiled back at me before I sighed.

"You know you're worried about it too."

"I am. But we're here and having a Pack dinner with our closest friends. You're allowed to breathe. I promise you. Nobody will blame you for smiling and laughing with your Pack."

We were speaking subvocally, low enough that only the two of us were part of our conversation. The others knew we were speaking but giving us privacy. Audrey was right. I needed to focus on the here and now, just for tonight.

That was what an Alpha did.

They were Pack.

And I needed to remember that.

"So, when did Gavin learn how to cook?" Adalyn

asked from the other side of the table, fluttering her eyelashes at us.

Gavin, Audrey's mate and the Tracker of the Aspens shrugged. "It's a roast. Not that hard. I've had a few decades to learn all over the world." He squeezed Audrey's hand, and I knew there was a lot of history in that gesture, but Audrey just smiled up at him.

"We know I can't cook a roast. I tried, and I burned it." She blushed before sighing. "But it's okay. My mate knows how to cook for us, so I'll never starve."

"You've had over eighty years on this earth, and you still don't know how to cook a roast?" Adalyn asked, and I knew that she was ribbing them to lower the tension in the room.

Audrey and I hadn't been the only ones having a tense conversation when we should have been focusing on coming together as a Pack.

"I could cook a decent roast, but I made the scalloped potatoes instead," Cruz said, as Steele just shook his head.

"You call those scalloped potatoes? I could do better."

My Heir and Enforcer began growling at one another, even though they were joking, and I turned to Audrey, narrowing my eyes. "Did you force them into making random jokes about dinner?"

"Maybe. But it is lightening the mood. And these

scalloped potatoes are delicious." She took a big bite and groaned happily as Cruz held up his hands in victory, and Steele flipped him off.

"Okay, I guess a cook-off is in the cards," Wren said quietly as she sipped her drink. Our Healer and lynx shifter just laughed softly as the others boasted about their favorite dishes, and my wolf padded around inside me, wanting to play and yet not knowing what to do.

I had so many years of not being part of a Pack or these friendships. I wasn't good at settling down when I needed to. It wasn't even all about the vampires and the attack where Skye had gotten hurt protecting me. That was only part of it. When I had been the Heir of the Pack, I hadn't done my duties. I had been forced into a cage and hidden away from the rest of the den, and now I was their leader, and I still felt like a fish out of water. Or maybe a wolf in sheep's clothing. Whatever metaphor worked with the situation where I was out of my depth.

My wolf wanted to settle, sit in my team's joyousness together as we grew our bonds closer, and yet it wasn't sure what to do, just like me.

The bond that connected me to a certain part of my Pack flared gently before it began to wrap warmth around my wolf, and I narrowed my eyes at the perpetrator.

The big polar bear just sat back in his chair, arms folded over his chest as he glared at me.

Hayes was the Omega of our Pack. It was his job to protect the emotional wellbeing of our den. Unless I locked my wolf, feelings, and body down completely, I couldn't hide all of my emotions from Hayes. There was just no way.

And Hayes didn't care if I wanted to hide from him. He would find a way to heal us, just like Wren found a way to heal our physical wounds, and how Steele was always thinking about ways to keep the Pack safe. Every single one of my team was doing their best in the roles that they were placed in by the moon goddess when the old hierarchy of the Aspen Pack had been wiped out.

Audrey and I were the only ones who remained, and the guilt that ate at me seemed everlasting.

Hayes leaned forward at the flare of emotion, and I sighed before nodding my head slightly at him and turning back to the rest of the conversation.

"I can make a decent chocolate cream pie," I put in, as everyone turned to me.

"You can make pie?" Audrey asked.

"I didn't know you could make pie," Adalyn growled. "Why did I not know that? Now I want pie. What do we have for dessert?" She turned to Cruz, who just snorted.

"I thought that was Gavin's job."

Gavin held up his hands. "Not even close."

"I made pie," Dara said, her eyes tired, but she still smiled. We needed the power of witches to add to the wards, just like we needed the soul strength of our Pack itself. But my father had killed so many of our witches and had used the dark magic of some of them in order to line his pockets with power.

Dara was putting too much of herself into the wards because, somehow, her death magic could counteract some of the vampire magic.

I needed to save her. *To help her.* Because she couldn't do this alone.

"What pie did you make?" I asked, my voice as soothing as possible.

"I made a checkerboard pie, as well as a banoffee pie."

Gavin held up his hands in triumph. "That's what I like to hear."

"I don't even know what those are," Adalyn grumbled.

"Don't worry, my dear, you'll enjoy them," Gavin said with a wink, and the hunter across the table just blushed.

"Stop flirting with me in front of your mate," she teased.

"If he were flirting with you, then I'd have to kill

him. So don't worry. He's just really happy for pie from England."

The fact that they could joke about the years that Gavin had spent in England—when he had been another person, had lost who he was—meant that the two of them were healing. Finding their path. Maybe I needed to try to do the same.

The others continued speaking, making plans for training, their routes for the next day, with that underlying tone of worry about what would happen next.

We finished eating and cleaned up before we dug into desserts, and I found out exactly what a banoffee pie was.

"Best pie ever."

Dara smiled softly. "I try."

I leaned forward, so only she could hear, and allowed my wolf out, not to scare her, but to show her I was there to protect her, just the way an Alpha should. "We're finding a way. This isn't all on you."

Her shoulders relaxed marginally and she leaned into me. I wrapped my arms around her shoulders and she sank into my side, still tense, but partially relaxed.

"I know you are. I'm sorry about what happened with the coven."

I held back my growl because I didn't want to scare her. It didn't matter that Dara was a harvester death witch and could literally hold death in her hand. She was still fragile, and I refused to hurt her with my anger.

"I'm just sorry that you have to deal with as much as you are. We'll figure out a way. There are good people in the coven. And good people outside of the coven, as well. We'll find people to help us. Because if we can find a way to help the den wards, we might be able to find magic to protect everyone. Not just ourselves."

Dara smiled wider then, her eyes brightening. "That's good. I like that idea."

"Where are Wynter and Lily?" I asked, speaking of her two friends that she was almost always with.

"Wynter's working, and Lily had a date." She wiggled her brows, and my eyes widened.

"Really? Someone I know?"

"She's keeping him secret for now because I think it's only their second date, and you know how we all get. A Pack of hens rather than wolves and bears and cats."

I tapped her nose with my finger. "And witches too."

"And witches too," she repeated. We were silent for a moment before she hugged me back tightly and stood up straight. "I can keep up with the wards for now. But we need to find another way soon." There was a worry in her words that echoed my thoughts, and I pulled her back again for a hard hug, kissed the top of her head, and took a step back.

"We'll find a way. We're working on it now. There

are a few Redwood witches that aren't mated in that are thinking about joining us."

The others in the room all paused to listen, and I spoke louder.

"Kade and I are discussing it because some of those witches are his family."

"Redwoods may become Aspens? That's a huge change," Audrey whispered.

There was another beat of silence, and I cleared my throat.

"I know. Because they wouldn't be Redwoods anymore, they would cut their bonds and become Aspens to help strengthen our Pack."

Cruz cleared his throat. "I know they do that with the Talons because of friendships, mating, and the way that those Packs are practically overlapping at this point."

"So doing that with us would be a clear line of full trust and alliance," Steele added, his face contemplative.

I nodded tightly. "I was going to tell you all later, but this is as good a time as any. We're making our way. Even if we become a huge Pack with four Alphas, we will find a way to protect ourselves and the humans around us." It was a promise I hoped I could keep, but from the trust in their gazes, it looked as if they believed me. So why did I feel like I hadn't earned that trust?

I tried my best to push the thoughts from my mind

as we discussed the intricate details of what would happen if we gained new members through the Redwoods, and subsequently the Talons. Once dinner was over, we dispersed, and I headed my way for my usual walk through the den.

The others needed to see me as Alpha. I would help them with whatever they needed. To carry a stack of food, I would do that. Did they need someone to hold a hammer and nail? I'd do that too.

Anything to show that I wasn't my father.

I still saw the inherent distrust on some gazes, those who only saw my father's features etched on my face, and not *me*.

By the time I finished my first circle, I wondered if I would walk on two feet or run on all fours to get to the other side of the den to meet with others outside of the den center.

Then a familiar floral scent hit me, and I found myself turning towards Skye.

My eyes widened as I looked at her, even as anger bubbled.

"What are you doing here?" I asked, my voice rougher than I had intended.

Skye raised a brow. "I had training with Novah," she answered, speaking of our Truth Seeker and friend.

"I wasn't aware you and Novah were friends."

"We aren't. We're acquaintances who could be

friends. Nico and I were here to train with her because she wanted someone to run with, and the last time I saw her she mentioned that she wanted more training. So we offered to help, just like Adalyn always offers to help us. Is that a problem?"

I glared at her, practically shaking.

"You sacrificed yourself for me. You got hurt because of me." My gaze went straight to her shoulder. "Is the scar gone?"

Her wolf was in her eyes, and she nodded tightly. "Yes. I'm fine. Leah was able to use the water magic to heal me. Even though she's not my Healer, it's okay. And, of course, I was going to push you out of the way to protect you. What the hell else was I supposed to do? You're the damn Alpha. I'm a soldier of no rank. Of course, I'm going to protect you."

"Don't talk about yourself that way. You don't get to sacrifice yourself for me."

"And you don't get to tell me what to do. You're not my Alpha."

"I don't want to see you hurt."

"Then stop getting into situations where vampires come at you."

I growled, took two steps toward her, and then crushed my mouth to hers before I thought better of it.

CHAPTER
SIX

Skye

My wolf pounced, heat settling in my belly as an unfamiliar flame scorched. He tasted of coffee and Chase. It was hard for me to think beyond that, to think beyond the feel of him.

I needed to do better. I needed to back away. I needed to not focus on him staying, to let my anger ride out. I should not have the hots for the Alpha of the Aspen Pack. And yet here I was, horny, gripping onto him as if he were my salvation, but he wasn't.

And he wasn't my mate.

Wouldn't I know? Wouldn't I know if the man with his tongue currently probing my mouth in the best way possible was my mate? He needed a strong person by his side. He needed the strength of a wolf with power. Or a human or a witch or any form of shifter that was better suited than me. He didn't need a casual fuck with the Redwood next door. And so I pulled myself away, remembering that we had been fighting.

He was so angry at me for trying to protect him. For getting hurt. Well, he would just have to deal with that because I wasn't about to back down.

I put my hands on his chest and pushed slightly. Ever so slightly, I didn't force him. I didn't moan or thrash. I just gently put pressure, and then he backed away, his chest heaving.

Because he *let* me do it.

Because he wouldn't *force* me.

Damn him.

"What was that?" I snapped, my wolf clawing at me —needing out. It didn't matter that I wasn't dominant or even close to being so. My wolf was ready to pounce, and it wanted him. This Alpha. The man I couldn't have.

"That was what I've wanted to do for far too long. You know that. It can't have been a surprise to you."

I stared at the man and shook my head. "It feels like a surprise, Chase. You were fighting with me. We haven't even *finished* that fight."

His eyes glowed gold, his wolf at the forefront. Only it wasn't the wolf I was in danger from in this moment, and we both knew it. "You're right. We haven't. So let's do so."

"Right here? In the middle of the forest where no one is around?"

"Do you really want our business witnessed?"

That made me pause, and I nodded. "You're right. I don't need the rest of the Pack to know that you're an idiot."

I hadn't meant for those words to be the first things that came from my mouth, but he blinked at me, raising a single eyebrow.

Why did he look so good doing that? Damn the man.

His eyes widened, the glow dimming as the man came forward, a smile peeking through the scowl. "Really? That's the way you're going to talk to me?"

"What do you expect? You are the Alpha of the Aspen Pack, Chase. Whatever those vampires wanted, they wanted to hurt you. They're using magic of their own making—dark magic that the witches apparently don't give crap about—and are aiming at you. This is the second time they've come directly at you."

"I'm well aware of that, Skye."

I ignored the way that my name sounded coming off his lips.

"I protected you. I was there on bodyguard duty. Not just for my Pack, but for everyone." I paused. "Even Henrick."

I sneered as I said his name, and Chase's lips turned into a smile. "I don't like him."

"Neither do I, but it's not like we have a choice about working with him."

"Perhaps we can find a choice."

"And perhaps that's above my paygrade," I teased.

"I don't know, Skye. You keep showing up to meetings here as help, protecting us. You deserve to know what's happening just like anyone else."

"Okay then, tell me what's happening between us."

I hadn't meant to say that either, and yet there was no taking the words back. Not when I needed to know.

Because that kiss? It hadn't come out of nowhere. We had been dancing around it for months now, and that was the problem.

"I want you."

That made me laugh. "Just like that. You're just going to say that as if it makes sense."

"You're a beautiful woman, Skye. Why wouldn't it make sense?"

"I don't know. How about we're from different Packs, different worlds. You're an Alpha."

"Is there something wrong with me being an Alpha?"

"No. You know that. But you need to find your mate." I swallowed hard at the pain that caused. Wondered why it hurt so much. "And we both know I'm not it."

He tilted his head and studied me. "So you're saying I can never have a relationship with anyone unless I know for a fact they are my mate? That no Alpha can? That's a lonely existence for an Alpha, don't you think?"

"I'm not saying that at all. But we both know that you're not my mate. Just like I'm not yours. And I don't want anyone to get the wrong impression that I'm trying to vie for an Alpha."

Chase threw his head back and laughed. He looked so handsome just then, and it was hard not to lean forward and bite him on his chin. Asshole.

"I don't appreciate the laughter."

"I'm not laughing at you. But at the thought that you think I'm such a catch that people will think that you are trying to what, con me? Con my wolf and the moon goddess herself? Skye. I'm allowed to be in a relationship, to scratch an itch, to fuck, to do all of that as long as it's with another consenting adult. I don't see the problem."

I pressed my thighs together, annoyed at the fact

that him saying the word "fuck" did such things to me. He inhaled, and I knew he was sensing my arousal.

"Stop it."

"Stop what? The fact that I can scent you? The fact that I know you're wet right now? That if I slid my hands underneath the waistband of your jeans, I'd feel you hot and ready for me?"

"Chase." I pressed my lips together, even tighter than I did my thighs, and exhaled.

"Skye. I'm not a catch. I'm Blade's son, the Alpha of a formerly—and still partially—broken Pack. It's not like I have women vying for me every day."

"Oh, that's nice. So since I'm the only one who happens to think you're hot, you can just imagine me falling for you easily?"

"So you think I'm hot?"

"Chase," I laughed.

"What? We both feel the attraction. We're wolves. We need skin to skin. We need that touch."

I paused and looked at him. "How long has it been for you?" I asked, worried about the answer. Not that he had been with someone, but that he *hadn't*.

"Far longer than I care to admit," he said through gritted teeth.

"So you and Audrey never...? You and Adalyn?" There wouldn't be jealousy for those two, not when I knew we needed touch. I just needed to know.

He snorted again. "No. Neither one. They're my friends."

"That's dangerous, Chase."

"It's dangerous that I didn't sleep with my friends?"

"No. It's dangerous that you haven't let off steam. You've got to be on edge all the time. Between this upcoming war or whatever's coming and all of the unknowns around it, in addition to your role as Alpha. You need sex."

He gave me a look, and I threw my hands in the air. "I'm not saying with me."

"Why not with you? Unless you don't want sex and I'm reading the situation wrong. If I am, then I'll walk away right now."

I began to pace, needing to breathe. "I know we as wolves need that skin to skin. That touch. That energy release. But you're an Alpha."

"I'm still a man, Skye. With most wolves and in any other Pack, we could comfort each other until we found our mates."

I froze, then turned to him. "*Comfort.*"

"Or scratch each other's itches. However you want to talk about it. If we go in both knowing we are not each other's mates, then it's fine. We can still be with one another and know that when the time comes and we find our mates, we walk away."

Something broke inside me, just slightly, a little ping

that echoed as it bounced around inside the hollowness of my chest.

Because he was so sure that he wasn't mine. That he couldn't be mine.

And yet, hadn't I just thought the same? That I wasn't good enough to be his.

Did he think I wasn't good enough for him?

It wasn't fated at first sight any longer, not with the changes the moon goddess had given us. Sometimes it took time and effort to figure out who your mate was.

He was sure, concrete in his statement that I wasn't his.

But you could be his for a moment.

I swallowed hard. "So we're friends with wolfie benefits until we find our forever. And then we walk away. No feelings, no attachments, nothing."

Chase was in front of me then as he slowly slid his fingers along my cheek. "You can't say no feelings. Friendly and comforting feelings are still feelings."

"I don't want to hurt you."

Nor did I want to be hurt.

He tucked my hair behind my ear, and I swallowed hard, my wolf howling, needing. "We're allowed to want."

"You never seem to let yourself do so."

He froze, and for a moment, I was afraid I had said

something wrong, and then he smiled softly. My wolf preened at the attention.

"You always surprise me, Skye."

"And how on earth do I do that?"

"By being you. By being fierce. And by seeming to see things that I don't realize are out there."

"So just friends. No more, no less."

"We can do that. There's attraction for sure. My wolf? It wants you."

Again, that familiar pain came up, but not in the way that my wolf wanted. I wasn't sure if he was my mate or if he could ever be. I felt as though my wolf needed time. And yet Chase? It was as if he *knew*.

So I would not fall in love with him. I would not fall in anything but lust. And I would let myself have this because I wasn't sure what I would do if I didn't.

In answer, I went to my tiptoes and pressed my lips to his.

He groaned against me and then slid his hand into my hair, wrapped it around his fist, and pulled. I let out a shocked gasp, my mouth parting, as he latched onto my neck, kissing and gently biting down. He didn't break the skin, didn't make a mate mark.

To create a full mating bond, one needed to complete two steps. The first being sex, where coming to completion in one way or another meant that you cemented the first step towards mating. The other was a mate mark. Each of the shifters would mark each other on the fleshy part of their shoulder where it met their neck, letting the whole world know that they were taken.

Claimed.

Both steps, one of human, one of shifter, completed the mating bond, and tied your soul to theirs for eternity.

With two shifters, mates' lives weren't forever bound together. So if one mate were to pass, the other mate would break, would grieve, but they wouldn't necessarily die. When one mated a witch, without special circumstances, their lives were forever connected to the ones with a longer lifespan. The same with humans, those humans that were altered and special at least, like my uncles. Humans who found their mates in shifters though, who didn't have a special, magical way of making it happen, were forced to turn into shifters. One of the only ways that the Supreme Alphas and Packs allowed changing to happen now. And that wasn't because we didn't want more shifters, but because we had to keep people safe. And if the government and humans thought that we were making too many shifters, it could bring out the activists and anti-shifter groups against us.

There was a sharp bite at my lip, and I looked up to see Chase glaring at me.

"Your mind is a thousand miles away and not on

this. On us." He tugged on my hair again. "Did I make a mistake?"

There was such a fragility in his tone, something I hadn't heard before, and I shook my head.

"No, I was letting my thoughts wander. I tend to do that."

"Then I better make sure you're paying attention to me."

And then his lips were on mine, and it was hard not to pay attention to him.

He kissed down my neck again, little bites of pleasure stinging along my skin. And when I did the same to him, he growled and then tugged on the bottom of my shirt. I took a step back and stripped in front of him, letting him watch me.

He might be the most dominant, but I wanted him to see that I had a semblance of control as well.

I wasn't wearing a bra, as I had shifted earlier and hadn't wanted to deal with the excess clothes, and so when my breasts fell, my nipples hard, his gaze grew gold and he let out a little snarl that went straight to my pussy.

"Skye. Oh, Skye." And then he was bent, one hand on a breast, his mouth on the other, as he sucked one nipple into his mouth. I groaned, my hand tangled in his hair as he sucked on my nipple, the sensations of tugging going straight to my core. He lavished attention onto my other breast, then switched back and forth, pulling and sucking and tugging until I couldn't breathe, couldn't think, and I was rubbing my thighs together. And when I came, it surprised us both, the scent of my arousal filling the air.

"I've never," I let out a breath, "actually had an orgasm from just someone touching my breasts before."

"Well, it looks like I'm a lucky man." And then I was somehow on the ground with him, both of us laughing as we tangled ourselves onto the ground, and he was protecting me from the fall. I let him do that. His need as an Alpha to protect was stronger than my desire to show I was dominant. Because I wasn't, and I knew what he needed. And that was time. I moved, and as I straddled him, topless, I blushed right to the tips of my breasts.

"Beautiful."

My long black hair skated around my shoulders. I leaned down, the sensation of the tips of my hair and his fingers caressing my nipples nearly too much.

"I need you."

I hadn't meant to say the words. Hadn't wanted them to be true, but from the pleased smile on Chase's face, he wanted that. Needed that. And I had to remember that this was an Alpha, a man who needed to protect and to be protected. I could be that for him. I wasn't so dominant that I needed to show the world that

I didn't need anyone. There was a side of me that wanted to be protected.

So maybe I should let him. He sat up, with me sitting in his lap, my legs wrapped around his body, and he cupped the back of my neck, his fingers in my hair, as he kissed me softly, exploring me. Our breaths came in pants, the pressure between us intensifying with each breath, with each touch and lick.

And then he was pulling off his shirt, and I was nearly swallowing my tongue at the sight of his body, the lean lines of his chest. He was thick and corded with muscle, and it was all I could do not to come right there.

We were still wearing our jeans, denim the only thing between us. I could feel the long line of his erection pressing against my core, and I swallowed hard, trying not to rotate my hips, to use the seam of my pants to get me off. He seemed to understand exactly what I was doing because he grinned and then moved to the side so we could strip off our jeans. It was hard to breathe, hard to think with him doing that. Because all I wanted to do was keep moving, to come, to feel him. I just had to remember to hold myself back.

To not want too much.

That would be what broke us both. I let out a sharp gasp as he continued to kiss me, and then we were both naked, him maneuvering me in just the right way. He lay me on the bed of leaves, my whole body shaking, and I looked up at him, hoping I was doing the right thing.

"You're so beautiful," he whispered.

"You're not so bad yourself." I was teasing with the words, but they were still true. Because he was gorgeous, all muscle and strength and Alpha. When I looked at him, I could barely hold in my own desires. The thing was, I didn't have to hold in my own desires. Not with him long and hard and thick and wanting between my legs. But he didn't tease me at my entrance, didn't plunge into me in one swift move even though I was hot and ready for him. Instead, he moved down my body, kissing me softly on the mouth, on my neck.

Along my body.

And then he was doing the same to my stomach, my breasts. Along my hips, and when he kissed between my thighs, gently probing my entrance with his tongue, I shook, my legs falling to the sides. He hummed along my wetness, spreading me as he kissed and sucked, biting down so gently that I nearly shot off the bed of leaves. But he didn't stop there. Instead, he kept sucking and licking and playing. Making me feel like I was everything. Just his in this moment. It didn't matter if anyone came down the path, who saw us right there. He wanted this just like I did. And that was all that mattered in that moment. All that would ever matter.

I came again, riding his face. He growled, shaking

between my knees. I couldn't breathe. I couldn't do anything except want and need, because that was the only thing that mattered to me. He was the only thing that mattered in this moment.

And when he hovered above me, between my legs, I reached between us gripping his cock.

"Chase."

"Are you ready?" he growled. His voice was all wolf. There was nothing of the man, the Alpha. No, this was the Alpha wolf. Not Chase, the man who was so concerned about my wellbeing that I felt as if I were cosseted. Loved.

No, this was the dominant wolf who needed.

And I was the wolf beneath him who wanted.

"Now. Don't make me wait." He laughed and took my hips, slid his hands below my thighs, pressed my legs up near my ears, and plunged into me in one deep thrust. The sensation made me scream, not in pain, but sheer bliss as I came again on him. He was buried to the hilt, stretching me in ways I hadn't thought possible, thick and ready and all fucking mine. And then he was moving, pounding me into the dirt, and all I could do was meet him thrust for thrust, needing and aching and wanting.

He didn't hold back. He didn't treat me like I was some gentle flower like all my other lovers had. No, he treated me like I was everything that he wanted and needed. I was everything for him, and that was all that mattered.

I moved for him, and when he continued to pound into me, I scratched at his arms, his legs, anything I could reach, just needing his touch, needing the sensation to keep going. He didn't push back, didn't pull away. Instead, he rolled, letting his body take the brunt of our assault. I couldn't hold back any longer. I rode him, my claws digging into his shoulders, knowing I was leaving wounds that would heal eventually. We were wolves, shifters. Not humans, not then. And that was all that mattered. We kept going, both of us shaking, needing, and this was all that mattered, all that was needed. He was everything, and I was his. I rode him hard, both of us shouting our desires, when my body tensed, my nipples hardened, I came. In that instance, it was everything and nothing and sensation and bliss. And my cunt clamped around his cock, both of us shouting, and then his hand was on the back of my neck, pulling me down for a bruising kiss. He kept his mouth on mine, his seed filling me, spurting inside of me, warm and hot and all man. I could barely breathe, could barely do anything.

But in the end it didn't matter.

Because right then, in this moment, I was his.

Claimed in every way possible except for the one way that mattered. And I didn't care. I was his for the moment, claimed and marked and sated.

We were friends, Alpha to wolf.

Man to woman.

But not mates. And as I came down from the high, I told myself to remember that.

We were not mates. We would never be.

But for now, I could have this.

CHAPTER
SEVEN

Chase

I LANDED FLAT ON MY BACK AND GLARED UP AT THE man on top of me.

"Seriously?"

Cole just grinned. "What? At least we now know who's more Alpha of the Alphas."

The poised and cautious Alpha of the Central Pack practically cackled as he got up and held out his hand to help me up. I glared at his outstretched palm before sliding my hand into his and jumping to my feet.

"Jerk. We both know who's the more dominant."

"Okay quick, whip them out, let's see." Cruz stood

to the side, hands on his hips. "That'll just make things easier, and we'll probably get a few spectators then."

I flipped my Heir off and looked over at Cole. "You surprised me with that outstretched kick. When did you learn that?"

Cole rubbed the back of his neck, studying my face. "I've been working with my brother-in-law from the Talons. He knows what he's doing."

"Damn, you're going to have to teach it to me." I rolled my shoulders back, annoyed. "I'm all stiff. It's pissing me off."

"Does that have anything to do with the scratch marks up and down your back and on your shoulders?" Cruz asked, teasing.

I glared at the other man, not bothering to blush or be ashamed. Because I'd been having the best damn sex of my life for the past week. Why would I be hiding or be ashamed? I shouldn't, so I wasn't even going to pretend.

The past week with Skye had been some of the best times of my life. Yes, the best sex, but just being able to be myself was worth any ribbing I was about to get. Not that anybody knew it was Skye. After the first time we washed off in the river, careful to keep our scents just to ourselves. It wasn't that we were ashamed —no, we were confident and sure of that—but we didn't need either one of our Packs, or the other two that were part of our alliance, to be nosing in our business.

And with the way that Cole and Cruz were both looking at me, like cats and wolves in cream? No, thanks.

"Seriously, who is she?" Cole asked as he went over to the other side of the gym and hydrated.

"Excuse me?" My wolf was too busy preening at Skye's attention to care what they were ribbing us about.

"Those claws aren't from fighting vampires or wolves. Tell us."

I flipped Cruz off. "No."

Cole leaned against the wall, grinning. "We could probably guess. Although the fact that you're hiding that scent, maybe I won't guess it."

Cruz shook his head. "If he's hiding it, that means we would be able to recognize it. It's not like you leave the den enough for you to find a human."

"Will you guys stop? Seriously. It's none of your business."

Both men looked at each other before they threw their heads back and laughed.

"That's enough. Get it all out of your system, and then I will kick your asses."

Cole just smiled. "I don't think so. You could try, but it's not going to happen."

I stared at the other two in front of me and knew I wanted to keep Skye to myself. Just for now. I hadn't expected her. That was probably the problem. Because I should have expected her. This was Skye. She was a fucking Jamenson. She was Pack royalty, and yet I knew there was something else beneath that surface. Something that said that she didn't believe she deserved to be where she was.

Perhaps it was because she was in an odd part of the hierarchy. She wasn't blessed by the goddess like some, nor was she in a high-ranking position. She floated in the middle, as if she wasn't sure where she should be. But she was always there, taking care of others. That was what I noticed. She took the jobs that helped others, even if she didn't feel that she had a right to be there.

That was the Skye I knew. The Skye I trusted.

And I didn't know what I was supposed to do with that. Because she wasn't my mate. She was a friend. A friend I was supposed to trust, be with, and yet not have forever with. Because one day, she would find her mate, and I would find mine. And I shouldn't be sad about the fact that I knew that no matter what, she wasn't my mate. She couldn't be.

"No, let's get back to work. No need to heckle."

"Oh, we're going to heckle." Cruz grinned. "I mean, do you even have the energy to continue? I assumed you'd already let off enough steam that maybe your old ass is a little tired now."

I flipped off my friend, then grinned over at Cole. "Show me that move."

The Central Alpha beamed. "You just want to be on your back again."

Cruz cleared his throat. "Yeah, but I don't think Cole is the one that he wants riding him."

I rolled my eyes, grateful we could laugh like this even when things were literal hell around us. "Guys. Seriously?"

"What? When's the last time we got to be idiots about shit like this?"

I frowned and nodded. "You're right. When was the last time either one of you guys got laid?"

"Okay, ow. That was uncalled for."

"Was it? Or was it exactly what is needed?"

This time Cruz flipped me off, but then Cole stood in front of me, glare on his face. "Okay, let's get you down."

"You say the sweetest things," I teased.

Cole flipped me off again, and then we were at it. "Okay, when they come at you, you're going to move like this." Cole showed the move, and I nodded tightly, knowing that the only reason the man could balance like that was because of his core strength and that he was a wolf. A human would probably fall and break their ankle.

These vampires could move so quickly one couldn't

follow them with the naked eye. They were stronger, faster, and deadlier than us. And that worried me. Because our Pack was strong, just not as strong as it used to be.

We would fix that though. We had to.

Before long, I was on my back again, probably bruised. I sat up and watched Cruz and Cole continue to train.

I liked trading out my training partners, keeping my beast on edge, and my skills at the ready. Cruz and Steele had been training with me for years, and Gavin was newer to it. I didn't train with Hayes that often, the big polar bear having his own issues. I worked with every single wolf, cat, human, witch, and bear in this Pack. Maybe not every week, but I tried my best.

Cole was new to my training life, but when we met just after each of us had been handed the mantle of Alpha, there had been an unspoken and later spoken truce between us. We didn't need to fight for territory, didn't need to fight for dominance.

We were in the same position, albeit shakier ones than the others.

Kade and Gideon, of the Redwoods and Talons respectively, had found their equilibrium together. Had fought side by side, had bled side by side. Their families had mated into one another, had blended their Packs so seamlessly that it was hard to see where one Pack ended and the other began.

One day the Aspens and the Centrals might be like that.

But first, we needed to increase our strength. The Central Pack was even smaller than the Aspen Pack, but we were trying.

It hurt to remember the time before. When we had been stronger, the rot had slipped deep inside our core. The Aspen Pack had been strong, a secretive force that had consolidated its power. But in order to make that happen, my father had used dark magic and the souls of his own in order to keep that power. He had wanted it to lord it out over the others and, in doing so, had killed countless.

I had been one of the lucky ones, if you could call it that. Because I had survived.

I still remembered every day of being inside that cage.

When the first disappearances in the Pack happened, I had tried to protect those weaker than me. But I hadn't been enough. Instead, I had been forced to stand back and watch my world shatter around me. I hadn't been enough. And my father had stuffed me into a cage, the metal grating. It had been too small for me, and I hadn't been able to sit up all the way. It had forced my body to heal incorrectly. To break when it shouldn't.

I had been weakened, far weaker than I should've been as the Heir of the Pack.

And throughout it all, even as I was slow to heal, weak to fight, and fading and failing, I had still felt the den within me. I had still known that I wasn't good enough. Because every time that someone died or been hurt or had screamed out in pain for help in my den, I had been locked in a cage and hadn't been able to do anything.

Someone snapped in front of my face, and I looked up to see Cruz. Cruz had been there through it all, had been Aspen for long enough to know that I was probably thinking things I shouldn't.

"Chase?"

I shook my head. "Sorry, letting my mind wander."

"I take it you're not thinking about the woman who's putting claw marks down your back," Cole asked as he drained his water.

"It's not a big deal. I need to get back to work. Thanks for the workout."

Cruz lowered his voice. "Are you talking to her about these things? Or Hayes? Anyone?"

I shook my head, knowing that there was no need to tell Skye my past. She knew enough, and that wasn't what we wanted our relationship to be about. Hayes knew enough as the Omega needed to for the health of the Pack, but I wasn't a fan of letting him work with my emotional bonds. The Pack needed him. I didn't. "I'm fine."

They both looked at me as if they knew I was lying. Because I was.

A subtle scent filled the room, and we turned as one to see Malissa walk into the room. She was petite, with strawberry blond hair and curves that could kill a man. She looked stunning in her business suit and her stilettos that put a good four inches on her tiny frame. Every time she walked, she swayed, and I didn't know if it was the heels or just her doing that.

"Hello, boys," she teased.

"Malissa," Cole said as he gave her a tight nod and leaned against the wall.

"Just the guys I wanted to see." She winked over at me, and my wolf just blinked right at her, wondering exactly why she was here.

She was nice, and my wolf liked her, but he was always a little worried. There was something off about how my wolf looked at Malissa. As if it recognized something, and so, therefore, I couldn't walk away. It was the what-if.

"What can we do for you, Malissa? How was work?"

She was an accountant down in the city. She worked for the den, but she also did a lot of her work outside of the den, making sure that she kept up with what was going on within the public. She was damn good at what she did, an asset to the den. Any man would be lucky to have her.

My thoughts just kept going to a woman with bright green eyes and dark black hair.

Not to the sunny woman with a kind smile in front of me.

"I just wanted to see if you wanted to do dinner." She was looking at me when she said it, then she pulled her gaze away and looked at the others. "All of you. I know you've had a hard time of it, and I made chicken pot pie."

My stomach rumbled, and Cruz sat up from the wall. "Your pot pie? When on earth did you have time for that?"

"I made it before I left this morning, instead of going for a run as I should have. But it'll be totally worth it. What do you say? There's enough for four." She smiled softly, and my wolf wanted her. Wanted to pad forward and see what she was about. Because she was interesting. Alluring.

I shook it off, wondering where that had come from because that wasn't my normal reaction to Malissa, and I didn't want it to be.

Was she my mate? That was the thing. I didn't know. I should have been able to tell, yet my wolf was intrigued.

Why did it feel like a betrayal?

"I'm sorry, I already have plans, but I'm sure the guys can."

"I have to head back to my den," Cole put in, looking oddly sad about it. "I promised my sister I would eat with her, and she's bringing some of the in-laws." He looked down at his phone and cursed. "Actually, I'm late."

Cruz came forward, a small smile on his face. "I'm in for pot pie, though I did promise Adalyn that I'd work with her later."

"Adalyn can come too. The more, the merrier. I'm just sorry that all of you won't be with us." She was staring directly at me, and I noticed Cole holding back a smile out of the corner of my eye.

I cleared my throat. "Thank you for the invite, Malissa."

"Anything for you. In fact, when you're done with your things, we should go for a walk. What do you think?"

The other two in the room slowly faded away, trying to give us privacy, and I didn't want to be here. "I'm meeting with someone tonight. But thank you, Malissa." I reached out and cupped her face like I would an Alpha to a Pack member, not sexual. She seemed to understand the difference, or at least I hoped she did, and she nodded softly.

"Thank you, Alpha. Just making sure you're okay."

"I am sad we're going to miss the pot pie, though. Right, Cole?" I looked over at Cole, who nodded.

"Seriously. My sister's cooking, so it's not going to be as good."

"I'm going to tell her you said that," Cruz added with a laugh. "Come on, Malissa. I need to go home and shower, but we can walk together."

"Sounds like a plan." She gave me one last longing look, and I felt it like a kick to the gut as she and Cruz walked away.

"So, you're taken?" Cole whispered.

"Yeah, I am. At least for now."

"So the person you're with, they're not your mate?"

My wolf whimpered, but I knew the truth. "No. She's not."

And I hated the finality in that tone.

"And Malissa isn't either." That wasn't a question, but I answered Cole anyway.

"I don't know, that's the problem. But we have more to worry about than my mating status. I just hope I didn't hurt her feelings."

"I don't think you did. You were fine, and both of you were up front. That's what I like about wolves. We try to be up front."

"That's the goal. I don't feel the mating urge, but I feel something. I just don't know what."

"I'm here if you need to talk. But I do need to go

back to the den, and it's going to take me a while to get there."

"Thanks for the training. And thanks for helping me not sound like such an asshole to turn her down."

Cole smiled. "Malissa is nice. And if she's yours, wouldn't it be good to know?"

Cole left finally, and I stood there in silence, knowing I was meeting Skye later because we were just supposed to comfort each other, to be each other's person until we found our mates.

But what if I had just found mine?

And what if I was making yet another mistake? One that I couldn't take back.

CHAPTER
EIGHT

Valac

AFTER YEARS OF STANDING IN THE SHADOWS, waiting for the wolves to finally do something with their power, it was time for them to realize who the true leaders were.

A gentle hand slid up his arm, down the open buttons of his shirt, to claw at his chest. Valac grinned, took the wrist near his mouth, and sank his fangs into her tender and pale skin.

His wife Sunny shivered in his arms, her eyes rolling back as he sank his fangs deeper, needing her blood, always her blood. Vampires needed to feed on other beings to survive, but this moment of play was all that he needed in this time and place because his Sun was his wife—his mate. And this could sustain him for far longer than others believed. And from the way that she shook in his arms, the scent of her arousal and musk filling his nostrils, he knew that this was exactly what she wanted.

"I wasn't expecting the bite, but wow, I do love you, husband."

Valac grinned, licked the holes on her wrist to seal them closed, and then left a soft kiss on her skin.

"So warm, sweet."

Sunny sighed dreamily into his side. "The delivery boy was just tasty enough. Kept me warm."

Valac grinned, knowing the myths of vampires being cold-blooded and needing the strength of mortals to survive were just that, myths. Nobody knew what they were like other than themselves, and that's how he preferred it. It was what he needed.

"Are you ready, darling?" Sunny asked, wrapping her arms around his waist. He returned the gesture around her shoulders and kissed the top of her head.

"I suppose it's time."

"We've given them enough time to rest. Though I am a little bit curious about the magic they're seemingly finding to use."

Valac scoffed. "They don't have the magic. They just think they do. Instead, all they have is a promise.

And we didn't even have to kill the coven in order for that power to weaken. They found a way to do it all on their own."

Sunny grinned up at him. "Isn't it interesting that the one power that they could have used to protect themselves, they lost without even knowing?"

"They'll learn too late. But until then, shall we finish the delivery?"

Sunny giggled, and Valac grinned.

"You're bad. Using a dead delivery boy as an actual delivery? Don't you think it's too on the nose?"

Valac shrugged. "We're leaving ten others. I think they'll get the hint. Children, husbands, wives, it's no matter. We will keep leaving the corpses of those they couldn't protect on their doorstep, and when they see who it is, they will find out exactly what they have lost."

"And it's time? For this step?"

"Do you dare question me?" a deep voice growled from behind them, and Valac's arms stiffened around his wife for a moment before he turned, a smooth and pleasant smile on his face.

"Malphas. You grace us with your presence." Valac and Sunny both bowed, their master's aura heady and daunting.

"This is a momentous step in our war. It is good for me to be here, so our compatriots know that they are not alone."

"Well, humans and others will soon be waiting for the Aspens. And when they find them, they'll know. And the next chess piece has been moved."

"Then make it so. I'm done waiting." At that, Malphas turned and walked off. Valac swallowed hard, annoyed with his own reaction.

"It's okay, baby. You can do this."

Valac looked down at his wife, his mate, his driving force, and nodded tightly. "Of course, we can. The others will soon realize who lurks behind the shadows and waits for them."

And with that, he and Sunny moved, nodding towards the soldiers as they carried the corpses to the strategic places around the Aspen border. The Aspen sentries were fast, diligent, and it wasn't easy, but in the end, the sentries only needed to find the bodies, the evidence.

They didn't need to find who'd left them.

Nor did they need to know why.

At least, not yet.

CHAPTER
NINE

Skye

TEETH LATCHED ONTO MY NECK, SCRAPING DOWN without breaking the skin, and I let out a shuddering breath, my hands sliding up Chase's back. He was shirtless, sweaty, and all I wanted to do was lick him up and bite down myself.

"You taste sweet. I like it," the Alpha rumbled against my skin and I smiled softly, my wolf padding around inside of me, happy, content, yet eager.

"I still have most of my clothes on, Alpha. Are you sure you even know what I taste like?" I teased.

Chase groaned against me and then slid his hands

around me, cupping my ass and lifting me with one swift movement.

I was strong. A shifter, an Anderson. A Jamenson. I knew strength. But the strength of his movement just then nearly felled me.

"I can't breathe," I whispered, squirming against him. He wore jeans, top button undone, riding low on his hips. I'd seen the deep Vs going on either side of his hips, angling towards what now pressed firmly against my core. My mouth had dropped open, and I had drooled just staring at him. I would've been embarrassed except for the fact that his eyes had gone straight to my lace-covered breasts, and he'd licked his lips, his gaze going gold, the wolf in control for that bare instant before he had reined it in again.

"We can fix that," he grumbled against me, and then his claws were out, slicing through the lace. I would've been annoyed, considering he kept destroying my bras, but considering I was already wet from just that movement, I decided I didn't mind. Instead I groaned, both of us clawing off the rest of our clothing until we stood naked in his home, my back pressed against the door.

I had been on the den lands in order to train with Adalyn. After a quick run with Chase, we snuck back here, needing the release.

It wasn't as if we could be circumspect about it. Shifters knew what we were doing, they could scent it after all, but nobody other than our close friends and family made jokes about it—because it was what shifters did. We needed touch—care. You could die from touch hunger if you weren't careful, and that was something that I would never let this Alpha do, and never let myself do, either.

A quick nip at my lip, and I glared up at Chase.

"What was that for?"

"Your thoughts weren't on me, and my cock is pressed against you. I'm very selfish."

I laughed, knowing that couldn't be further from the truth. This was Chase. He was not a selfish lover, nor a selfish Alpha. He was so much in the other direction that it was a little startling and worrying about what he would do if someone asked him for everything.

Not that I would ever be that person.

I quickly pushed those thoughts from my mind and went back to kissing him before we fell onto the floor in a tumble, my hand around his cock, stroking him, his lips on my breasts.

When he slid his hand between my folds, slicking my wetness over my clit, I arched my back, my breasts pressing against his face as he continued to suck and tease. I could barely reach him to stroke him. All I could focus on was him. And when he was deep inside me, stretching me with one deep thrust, I moaned, my claws digging into his shoulders. I scented blood and winced, pulling my claws back out of his skin.

"Sorry," I whispered as he moved oh so achingly slow in and out of me.

Chase just grinned as if he was the cat with a canary.

"Keep doing it. I like you losing control. Your claws in me."

He didn't mention marking him, and I understood. Because while I was technically marking him, to say it would bring in the mate question, and that was something that I was not. Because he knew. He was so sure of it. So I would be sure of it, too.

I quickly buried those thoughts as he gripped my hips, a bruising force that I knew would leave marks on me. Marks that I needed—craved. And then his mouth was on mine, and there were no more thoughts—just him and me, and that sweet slickness that was each other. And when I came, I groaned, my entire body shaking, before he pulled out and flipped me to my hands and knees. I laughed before a breath was pulled from me. He thrust back in me, pounding hard and fast, just shocked gasps, inhalations of breath as he kept going, his claws digging into my hips, my claws digging into the wood floor. I would leave grooves there, ones he would see later and think of me, and a little part of me smiled. The rest of me knew it was probably a mistake. But I didn't care.

I couldn't care.

And then I came again, and he was roaring, the howl ripped from his throat as he came inside me, filling me, hot and warm.

We fell together in a tangle of limbs, even as his hand was still on my clit, rubbing as if he wanted to ensure that I came one more time. I tried to push his hand away from me, but he just kept going. Even as he was softening inside me, he kept rubbing and touching and bringing me to completion one more time.

My whole body ached, not just from being fully sated and stunned, but also from the training I had done for most of the morning before this. I could barely breathe, think, and yet I was in his arms.

I pushed those thoughts away once more. Because I wasn't in his arms. We were just friends, caring for one another. Nothing more.

"Wow," I whispered, my voice filled with soft laughter.

Chase kissed my shoulder, just a gentle brush of lips on my skin, and I let out a soft breath, that clutch in my heart familiar, painful.

"Wow's a good word. I like wow."

I laughed and snuggled into him with my butt pressed to his body.

"Well, you do know how to make a girl smile." I winked even though he didn't see me, but since I could hear the laughter in my voice, I was sure he understood.

"I try." He slowly slid out of me, and I tried not to feel bereft at the loss. There was something seriously wrong with me if I was missing him already. I had to keep better control over this. This was Chase, after all. We were friends, helping one another. There didn't need to be anything more.

"When do you need to leave?" he asked as we cleaned up our clothes pile and headed to the bathroom. Chase turned on the water, and I didn't even think he realized what he was doing, caring for me—that Alpha need to protect someone more submissive than him.

"I have dinner with my family tonight, and then I'm on patrol later."

"On the Redwood Den?" he asked, and I nodded, following him into the shower. He pressed his back to the water, taking its brunt before the temperature was comfortable. I didn't know why I knew that, other than that was such a Chase thing to do. Caring for me even though he didn't even realize he was doing it.

I reached for the body wash, put some in my hands, and began to rub it all over his chest and a little bit lower. He groaned and steadied my hands.

"If you do that, we're both going to be in this shower for far too long, and we have meetings."

I smiled, went to my tiptoes, and kissed him softly. I pushed away any emotion that I could feel in that moment, other than friendship, and smiled against his lips.

"I'm just making sure you're clean. I promise I won't go down on my knees and suck you off. Again."

"You are a cruel woman. I like it." He bit my lip again, and my wolf relished the sting before we washed each other's bodies and cleaned off the sweat and evidence of what we had done. I wasn't sure we would be able to hide the scent, because we weren't trying to anymore, and we were deep into each other's skin at this point, just like any friends with touching benefits would be.

Nobody had commented that I wasn't good enough for an Alpha, that I was making a mistake. Then again, I didn't think they would. Not when they knew as much as I did that this wasn't forever. It was just for now.

"What put that sadness in your gaze?" Chase asked, after the water was off and we had wrapped towels around each other. He trailed his fingers over my cheek, and I shrugged, putting on that brave face that I was so good at.

"Just thinking about all I have to do. I'm running late," I said as I looked at the clock above the towel rack.

"So am I. But I don't regret it."

I smiled then, my heart far too full. "Neither do I.

But I do have to go get dressed. So you can't look at me naked, or I'm going to get distracted."

He reached out, sliding his hand underneath my towel to grip my ass. I groaned as he slid his fingers between my legs, sliding over my wetness.

"Chase," I growled.

"Just making sure you're wet for me. I like it."

"Possessive much?" I asked.

"Maybe." He winked and put his hands half in between my legs, and I quickly turned, moving towards my clothes after he sucked on his fingers.

I knew that he could scent my arousal, and I would drench my panties as soon as I put them on.

That damn man knew what he was doing, and I kind of hated him.

We dressed separately and I kissed him goodbye, making my way to my vehicle at the edge of the den territory. I didn't see anybody that I really knew on my way there, and I was grateful. My thoughts were in a whirlwind, and I needed to focus. It was just hard to do so when all I could think about was Chase.

I needed to be better than that, because Chase was just a friend.

And if I kept telling myself that, maybe I would remember.

It took over an hour to get home, as the dens were spread out enough that we each had our own territory.

But, thankfully, my parents' home in the den was on the southernmost part of the territory, so it wasn't as far of a drive as it could have been.

I slid past the wards, that familiar magic warm and inviting as I entered Redwood land, and then pulled up to my parents' home and noted that I was the last to arrive.

Edward and Brendan were already on the porch, laughing at something, and as they looked at me, my big brother raised a brow.

"Well, did you have fun *training*?" he asked, emphasizing that word.

I flipped him off as Brendan laughed.

"Aw, you're so sweet. I see you tried to shower before you came to family dinner. I can still scent him, though," Brendan added.

"Be nice to your sister," Mom said from the door. Cailin Jamenson Anderson was gorgeous, with long dark hair, almost blue it was so black. Her piercing green eyes saw everything, and always had.

My mother was everything to me. She was exactly who I had always wanted to be growing up. A force of nature, even without a place in the hierarchy. She didn't need a title in order to have the strength she did. The same with my father, as Logan Anderson had been through hell and back before he had joined the Redwoods. The story of my parents' courtship and mating was one of legend, and it always made me smile when they told it to me. They had nearly died for each other countless times in order to protect our family and our future.

And yet here I was, playing with an Alpha I knew I could never have.

I wanted that courtship, that love, and the fierce mating bond that my parents shared. That all of my family seemed to be able to find.

And I knew I wasn't going to be able to.

At that sad thought, I went straight into my mother's arms without a word. My brothers seemed to have noticed something was wrong, or at least off, with me, and they didn't tease me anymore.

When my mom kissed the top of my head, I was reminded that she was still taller than me despite the fact that I wasn't petite by any means.

"How was training with the Aspens?" she asked, and I knew there was more to that question than just training. But she wouldn't ask unless I was ready to answer. And because I wasn't, I just shrugged.

"Pretty good. Adalyn's wonderful."

"Just Adalyn?" My dad asked from the kitchen as his gaze narrowed.

"Dad."

Logan Anderson just shrugged. "Sorry. You're my

baby girl. It's what I'm going to do. If I have to go take down an Alpha, I will."

"Logan," Mom snapped, even though her eyes were full of laughter.

"Oh, dinner and a show? I'm glad that I'm invited," Nico said from the doorway.

I turned to my cousin and raised a brow.

"Did I know you were coming?" I asked, fluttering my eyelashes.

"No, but I was training with Edward most of the day, and I'm on your patrol route tonight. Your parents invited me to dinner."

"Oh, cousin, let's go eat. And don't be mean." I narrowed my eyes at him, but he just grinned and winked.

Sometimes it was like having forty brothers instead of just two. That was us, Redwoods. We were family through and through.

I was a Redwood. No matter who I was currently sleeping with. I was a Redwood.

And I didn't need to think about a pull that felt awkward and unwieldy, to a den, a Pack, and an Alpha that weren't mine.

Dinner was a loud affair, and although we were one of the smallest sets of families within the den, we were still rowdy. My parents sat together, lovingly looking at each other between bites, and I ignored that pang of jealousy within me.

My brothers teased me, but they teased each other just as much. I could give as much as I could take, and I loved this.

I helped wash the dishes, and then Nico and I left the den territory to patrol the outside perimeter. A familiar scent carried on the breeze and I looked up, waving at Adalyn as she came forward. She would be on patrol with us. Nico looked up, his wolf in his gaze before he waved as well.

"Do you want to talk about it?" Nico asked, and I shook my head.

"No, I don't really want to." I wasn't going to lie to him or anyone that I wasn't thinking about something. But I also didn't need to tell them everything. At least not yet, while I was still thinking.

"Okay, but if you want to talk, I'm here."

"I know. Thank you."

"And thank you for going on this patrol with me," he said after a minute, and I frowned.

"Why wouldn't I?"

"Because you've been training all morning, and you could have easily gotten out of your duty tonight."

I shook my head. "No, I couldn't have. It is my duty. I go where I am needed."

Even if I didn't have the title or strength that most everyone else did in my position.

I wasn't really enjoying the fact that I was feeling so down on myself, so I pushed those thoughts away and kept my attention on the outside perimeter. Something just felt off tonight, and I didn't think it was my own emotions. Adalyn moved to our side, silent in her strength as she studied the area around us.

"You feel it too?" Nico asked, and I looked up at him, his dark brown hair pulled back from his face in a small ponytail. It was far too long for him, and I knew he didn't like it, but he was annoying his brothers with the haircut.

"I don't know. Something just feels weird."

Adalyn cursed under her breath. "I'm glad it's not just me. And considering I don't have the same connection to this part of the land as you do, I don't like the feel of it."

Before either one of us could say anything more, something came out of the bushes.

Nico called out an alert, a quick howl that I knew would let the others know where we were if something was coming.

"Vampire?" I asked, frowning.

Nico scowled. "Maybe? Fuck, I don't know."

It was tall, at least six foot five, and had once been a person. But now it looked like a half-shifter, half-human *thing*. It was a monster and fast. Drool slid from one side of its mouth, its fangs elongated.

"Oh my God," I whispered as my claws flew out of my skin.

"I don't think we're going to be able to keep this one alive," Nico whispered. We were on the same page, wanting to know what this magic was. What if this person was forced into this? We didn't want to kill them if we didn't have to.

The thing in front of us sliced out, its claws long, far too long. It didn't look like a vampire or a shifter. And not a human. It was something *other*. And it was scary.

It sliced out again, growling, but I saw the panic in its gaze.

The pain.

It struck out at me and I ducked, kicking it in the leg. It kept coming, slicing, punching. It got Nico in the chest but luckily didn't break the skin. Nico cursed and pushed down at the thing.

"Try to incapacitate it."

Adalyn jumped on its back, trying to pin it with Nico, but the thing was *strong*.

"It looks like it's in pain!" I called out, my wolf whimpering in its own horror at the sight.

I scented blood and saw the wound on the monster's side. It was dying. Someone had gutted it before it had even come to us.

Someone had led it here.

To the Redwood lands, and not the Aspens.

It fought us until it finally dropped after a quick hit from Nico and a kick from me. I saw the agony in the monster's gaze, it whispered one word, and then it fell dead at our feet without us even doing it.

"It was dead before it even came to us," Nico muttered as we looked down at the thing in front of us. There were footsteps as others ran to us, but I knelt down in front of the thing that had once been human, at its panic-stretched gaze, and let out a shocked gasp.

"Gold, Nico. His eyes had been glowing gold."

My cousin looked down at me and then at the others who came to our side, Adalyn muttering under her breath as she glared at the unfortunate soul at our feet.

Nico growled. "He was a shifter. Before."

My wolf panicked, pawing at me, and I swallowed hard.

It was a hybrid. Formerly shifter, turned vampire.

Was this what happened when a shifter turned vampire? Or when something went wrong? I didn't have the answers, but as the others came, my wolf panicked, and I knew that things had just changed. Again.

CHAPTER
TEN

Chase

"A HYBRID," I SAID SLOWLY, TRYING TO COME TO terms with what Skye and the others had told me.

Steele stood in front of me, shaking his head. "That's what they're calling it. A hybrid of wolf and vampire."

"How do they think it was made?" I asked, kind of shaking my head. "Not that any of us truly know the answer."

"It could be that this is what happens once we are bit and nearly die, or magic, or whatever else they use. If Jagger was honest, about how he told us how humans were made into vampires, perhaps it's a completely different process for shifters."

My wolf prowled inside me. "All we do is come up with more questions, more unknowns. And all we can do is wait for the next shoe to drop. I hate this."

My Enforcer looked at me but didn't say anything. I could feel his wolf pacing beneath the surface as if he had questions, but what was either of us supposed to say?

"Out with it," I said after a moment, knowing Steele needed to at least let something out.

"This is not your fault. We're going to figure this out. We always do."

I paused, a growl sliding through. "We've been through this before? Something *exactly* like this that we can figure out?"

"I'm not saying that," Steele said, his lips forming a smile. It was rare to see Steele smile these days. But I appreciated it.

"We barely survived our war before. And that was when it was just wolf against wolf. Magic against cat and bear."

"The Redwoods defeated the demon before. The Talons helped defeat the government and the rogue agents, so we shifters could breathe in a semblance of peace. We can do this."

"I've never heard you be so encouraging before. You almost sound like Audrey these days."

That made Steele snort, and I couldn't help but let my own smile cross my face.

"Audrey spends all her time cleaning up after the rest of us as we're trying to figure out how the hell we run this Pack. She's the only one with any form of experience and, at some point, I guess we should let her live happily mated with Gavin."

"At some point. Although, if anyone of us is more positive than her up here, it's Wren, or maybe even Hayes."

Steele gave me a dry look. "If that big grumpy-ass polar bear of an Omega is our positive encouragement for this Pack of ours, we are deeply in trouble."

I sighed and set my hands on my hips. "Well, you aren't telling me something I don't know."

"I'm not saying we're in trouble. Other than we are."

"Is that my friend speaking? Or the Enforcer of the Aspen Pack?"

"Both and you know it, my friend. We need to meet with the elders. Is Cole coming?"

"He's on his way. They don't have elders as we do."

"Because their former Alpha killed the rest of them. But they're finding their way now. Just like we are."

"We don't have many elders left, Steele. And I don't think they trust me."

"Then lead. Just like you've been doing. They'll follow. You're Alpha. They'll follow."

"I don't know. But I need to get my head out of my ass and work on this."

"Is Skye coming over?"

I blinked at the other man, kind of shaking my head. "You want to talk about this now?"

Steele threw his hands up in the air. "No, not really. All I was thinking was that it might be nice if she was here to go over what she saw. Nico too."

"Adalyn will be here. Nico and Skye are back with the Redwoods. Their Healer's going over the body. They've sent over the results that they have so far and will send over more once they have them."

"See, we're already working together. You're forcing me to be optimistic, and I'm not a fan of that."

I laughed. I couldn't help it. "Yes. We'll let you get back to your normal assholish self. That will help things."

"You're a jerk. But I love you like a brother."

"Thanks for that. I appreciate it."

"I know you do. We're going to be okay. We have to be."

"There's that optimism again. I'm a little afraid."

"Well, the rest of the core team is usually a little peppier than me. I'll let them take over managing your mood later."

"Thanks for that," I said dryly, and we made our way towards the northern end of the den.

Though we could sustain ourselves within the den—with jobs and schools and farming and trade—we did have people that lived outside the den. We weren't a hidden compound anymore, not like what my father had wanted. And although the danger was high and the threat real with the vampires, and now perhaps these so-called hybrids, we still had people who worked and lived outside the den within the cities, and we had some of our soldiers stationed there. They kept their eyes and ears piqued so that we could understand what was happening around us. All of the Packs did that, some more than others because they had the forces to do so. We were just now replenishing after hiding for so long, so it was good to find a way to help the alliance rather than just being dependent on them.

Within that aspect, though, our elders—of whom we had few we had left—needed us to be strong. They weren't my council, nor were they the former elders who had once reigned as my father's council and had been murdered in their sleep. These were the wolves that were secluded because they wanted to be. They had the experience of life, and through loss or tragedy, they had secluded themselves.

They were the ones that I spoke to for guidance, along with the other Alphas and leaders.

They were far older than me, and yet I knew they were only the tip of the iceberg when it came to the lore and life-lessons learned that some of the other Packs had.

Cole met us at the edge of the elders' territory within the den, and I nodded at the other Alpha.

It was odd to think that this man was my friend so easily. We probably would have taken a while to find our footing around each other in any other circumstance, to realize that we could be friends without battling out for land, territory, and power.

But both of us were in the process of rebuilding, struggling in ways that only each other could understand.

There was no need to fight one another to see who was more powerful, more dominant, more Alpha.

Our wolves were content in knowing that we had an ally.

While things were different with Kade and Gideon of the Redwoods and Talons, respectively, because of their own legacies, Cole and I were friends learning to lead.

Young Alphas trying not to fail.

"Well, I see the weight on your shoulders hasn't lessened any," Cole said after a moment, and Steele looked between us, shook his head, and made his way towards the elders' area. I could scent the others had already arrived, so Cole and I would be the last ones to walk in.

"Are you okay?" Cole asked, his voice a whisper.

I looked at the other man and nodded.

"I'm fine. How are you?"

"You say that as if I should know what the hell I'm doing," the Central Alpha said with a laugh.

"I never know what I'm doing," I teased.

"Hybrids now? Fuck, Chase. I don't think we're going to get a break anytime soon."

"I don't either. Are your wards good?" I asked, knowing that with any other Alpha I wouldn't come out and ask that. Even among allies and friends, such as Kade and Gideon. We were friends that had to trust one another because we needed to know our own weaknesses. And if we didn't learn the other's weakness, how would we realize if we had a similar shortcoming?

Cole nodded. "As good as they can be, but gaining power."

"Let's get in there," I said after a moment.

"Okay. What are you hoping to get out of them?" Cole asked as we made our way towards the elder circle.

"Honestly? I don't know."

"Well, that's something good to know," Cole laughed.

"They might have seen something come up or just have experience. And, honestly, I need to tell them what

I know. I need my Pack to trust me. And that means not keeping secrets like my father did."

Cole swallowed hard. "I tell my Pack everything that I can. I don't want them to be scared, but those we call elders, those that aren't that much older than me, they're scared. They're always scared."

"But you protect them. You show your strength."

Cole looked down at his hands, as if seeing something that wasn't there. I didn't ask. It wasn't my place. We all had our own burdens, our own paths and tragedies. Cole had his, and maybe one day, he would tell me. And maybe one day I would tell him mine.

It was odd to think the only person that I had even considered telling recently was Skye. I didn't know why. Why should I be able to trust her when I knew she could never be mine?

I quickly pushed those thoughts from my mind, knowing now wasn't time.

"Those that protected us, the kids that were born into the Centrals, and then right after? They were the submissives. The maternals had been beaten and broken. There hadn't been dominants to protect us. I don't know how they did it, other than pure strength of will and heart. And now I'm here to protect them. The Redwoods and the Talons protect us, too, but you and I are trying to find our footing, and we will. And if that includes asking the elders for help, even when we know that they might not have anything for us other than recrimination and fear, that's something we must do as Alphas."

And that was why Cole and I were friends. He understood exactly what we needed to do, even though others might not understand.

My team was already waiting for me at the circle, the small grouping of elders at the circle sitting around a small campfire, talking amongst themselves.

Because wolves didn't age physically like humans and witches did, the five elder wolves looked my age. Some were a little more ragged than others, but they didn't look as if they had lived any longer than a few decades. But they were all over a century, most around five centuries. They had experience, had survived my father, and hadn't gone to his side.

I had to trust that was good enough.

Dorian, the leader of the elders, looked up at me, his eyes gold with his wolf.

"You're here, with the young Alpha."

Cole smiled, looking sweet as can be and not like the Alpha of a Pack.

"Thank you for letting me join you for this meeting."

"Of course, of course," Dorian said as he waved us off as if Cole and I weren't the two leaders.

"Let's sit and discuss these hybrids. And what they are, and what exactly you plan to do about it."

Audrey met my gaze over Dorian's head and winced.

Her mate Gavin stood by her side, and I had a feeling that this meeting wasn't going to go well. The problem was that these elders didn't trust me. Each of them saw my father in me. I could feel it across the Pack bonds. They didn't trust who I was, and there was no changing that.

Cruz and Steele stood off to the side as if ready to pounce in protection. Wren and Hayes sat next to two of the other elders, each of them working their own magic. One of the female elder wolves had cut her palm, and Wren was healing it. Hayes pushed out his magic of emotions, healing those he could along those bonds. Even though I never wanted him to see deep inside me, that was what an Omega did.

Adalyn was the only one there not of the hierarchy, and it was for a good reason. She had seen the hybrids, and we needed to know what she had uncovered.

"Well then, tell us," Dorian said, his voice bitter. Dorian hadn't liked my father even before he had lost his mate because of Blade. No wonder the man didn't like me.

I knew that Steele and the others wanted to growl at Dorian for daring to speak to me like that, but I held them all off, using my own dominance to do so. I couldn't let them push at Dorian and the others for their own views on me. I had to earn their respect. Not just because the moon goddess had blessed me. No, I had to do it as Alpha and as man.

And as Blade's son.

"Come on over, take a seat near me," Adalyn said. Cole gave me a look, one that I couldn't read, and went to sit by the hunter. I sat on her other side, my gaze on Dorian, wondering what he was going to say.

"What did you see?" Cole asked, his voice low, and I was grateful to him for starting this conversation.

I could see the distrust in Dorian's gaze, probably because he didn't want another Alpha here. But this was my choice, and I was finding my way, just like the rest of us.

"Well, it looked like a monster." Adalyn shuddered, and I saw Hayes reach out, as if to help, but Adalyn held up her hand.

"Don't you worry, Omega. I'm fine. I kind of need this rage right now."

I saw the respect in Dorian's gaze before the elder wiped it away, and both Hayes and the others leaned back, respecting Adalyn's fierce strength.

"It was half-shifter, half-vampire. Or, at least it looked like it was shifting between the two and couldn't make a decision, or the turn had gone wrong. I'm not sure, but we were outside the Redwood Pack den, training, when something let it out there."

"They knew you were going to be there," Cole said, speaking my own thoughts.

"I'm not sure. It could have just wanted to go at anybody who was near the den. We were along the patrol lines, so we were never alone for long. The only reason we were outside the den was because Skye and Nico had patrol later. And it's a good field to train in."

"And you're going to figure out what these are?" Dorian asked, after Adalyn went on into detail about how the fight had occurred.

I didn't like the idea that Skye, Nico, and Adalyn had nearly been hurt because of it. And I didn't like the fact that my wolf was pushing me to check on Skye. I had texted her earlier to make sure she was okay, and while she had said yes, the texts had been curt. But they needed to be. Because Skye wasn't mine. And I wasn't her Alpha. Just her lover—for now.

"We're working on it. Have you ever heard of anything like this?" I asked the elders.

They all shook their head, but Dorian narrowed his gaze at me.

"I do find it odd that the woman that smells of you found it," Dorian said after a moment.

Adalyn stiffened, but I held up my hand.

"Excuse me?"

"That Redwood. One not Pack. Just like he is not Pack," Dorian said as he waved towards Cole.

"They are friends. Allies."

"They aren't Pack," Dorian snapped.

"Watch your tone, elder," Audrey said calmly, far too calmly. But she was the Beta, and it was her job to see to the needs of those within the den. And to make sure that everyone knew who was Alpha.

"Dorian, would you like to go for a walk?" Cruz asked.

He held part of the mantle that I did, and I knew he could feel the tension along the Pack bonds like I could. Our Pack didn't trust our hierarchy as well as it should. With good reason, if you included what had happened in the past. But, now, we were all trying our best to be the strength that they needed us to be.

"You bring in others, outsiders. And that wolf that scents of you found this so-called hybrid. I just find it a bit circumspect."

The silence was so poignant in that moment, I could hear the crickets begin their song before they quieted as well. There was a wolf on the prowl, and it wasn't the elder in front of me.

My wolf growled, scraping at me. How dare this man speak of Skye like that? How dare he speak of all of them like that?

I stood up slowly, and I saw the fear in the other

man's gaze. He was scared. Perhaps of the vampires, of the coming threat.

But he was also scared of me.

And the blood in my veins.

And just like that, my wolf drew back as if ice water had been dumped on us.

"Dorian. We will find out what is attacking us. The Redwoods, Skye, Cole, all of them, they are our friends and allies. These battles are far bigger than one Pack, and we need this alliance."

"That is what your father said when he went to the dark witches for power. When he held us in our bonds."

"Enough," Cruz growled, his voice low, dangerous.

Cruz was far more dangerous than anyone else knew, but I held up my hand, calming his wolf. I had to. I looked over at Hayes, and the polar bear nodded. He would ease some of the tension using his powers as Omega. But I didn't want him to manipulate everyone too far. There was only so much we could do without causing harm.

I knelt in front of Dorian, but I didn't back down, didn't lower my gaze.

"We came to you to tell you what we know and ask for aid. If you do not know anything, I understand. These threats are new. But we will fight, and we will win. Because that is who we are. I am not my father." Yet, those words felt like a lie. "I need to trust my

Pack. And I need them to know that they can trust me."

"You ask for much, *Alpha*."

He put emphasis on the last word, and I let it go. For now. With a sigh, I reached out and gripped his shoulder slightly to show I understood. Even though I didn't. Dorian let his gaze lower, and I sighed before I stood up and looked at the others.

"We have patrols to do. Training to work on. Let's go."

I turned my back to them, knowing that if Dorian somehow found it in his strength to attack me, the others would stop him. And I would as well.

My Pack didn't trust me. Because of who my father was. And, no matter what I did around the den, no matter who I tried to protect, I wasn't going to be good enough.

I just needed to remember that.

CHAPTER
ELEVEN

Chase

THE WOLF PUP IN FRONT OF ME TUMBLED HEAD over tail. I shook my head, crouching in front of him as I helped the baby stand on all fours. It yipped at me and I met his gaze, the little puppy licking at my nose.

"Okay, Jesse. Let's get better at that whole pouncing thing."

Honor and Monday, two other pups, came bouncing around my feet, yipping and nipping at my ankles, as if I wasn't the Alpha of their Pack and just another play-mate. I needed to deal with human problems soon, so I couldn't shift and play with them, much to our mutual disappointment.

"Now, let's practice being sneaky. Wolves can be sneaky."

Audrey rolled her eyes, her arms folded over her chest. "Cats are far sneakier. Let me show these little puppies how to be lion sneaky."

The wolf pups looked between us, little wolf smiles on their faces.

This was one of my favorite things about being Alpha. They trusted me inherently. There was no memory of who I had once been, of who my father had been. Yes, they had been alive when Blade was Alpha, but they didn't remember him or the pain. Instead, they just remembered *me*.

Monday climbed up my leg, her claws safely hidden away, making it hard for her. I smiled and lifted her so she wouldn't hurt herself and cuddled her to my chest. She grumbled in thanks and then tucked herself into my neck and shoulders, promptly going to sleep.

I couldn't help but laugh, trying to be quiet about it so I wouldn't wake her. I sat cross-legged on the ground, both Jesse and Honor crawling into my lap to sleep. They had played hard, among themselves with the soccer ball, and then with me learning to pounce, and were all tuckered out quickly. Jesse slept with his little mouth open, panting, his tongue hanging out, and I held back a smile, watching the three wolf pups as if they were my own. Their father was out on patrol, their mother working in the city, so Audrey was on babysitting duty and had thankfully let me tag along to play while Gavin was on patrol.

"Makes you want one of your own, doesn't it?" Audrey asked, a soft smile on her face as she leaned forward and ran her fingers over Honor's nose.

I shrugged, the action smooth and gentle so I wouldn't jostle the three miscreants tangled over me.

"It sometimes does. Though I'm not quite ready for something like that."

"I suppose mating is something that the Alpha needs to do first."

I heard the pointed note in her words and shook my head. "Yes, although with the new mating guidelines, with the moon goddess changing things to save us, who knows. Maybe you don't need a mate first to have a baby."

Audrey's eyes widened very big. "That would be a game changer, wouldn't it?"

I shook my head and looked down at the babies. "They're growing up in a safe Pack. I need to make sure we keep it that way."

Others were rolling around, doing their work for the day, training, or just moving around like normal. I could feel their stares on me, some because they wanted to see their Alpha, some because I was Blade's son. I hated the fact that I couldn't even tell the difference between the two stares.

"Are you and Gavin thinking about pups or cubs?" I asked.

Audrey's eyes widened and she snorted. "Not any time soon. We are newly mated, for the second time. It is nice just to be each other's person for a while."

She paused, looking down at the sleeping wolf pups in my lap. "And, honestly, with the vampires attacking our den, I don't want to be in the vulnerable position of being pregnant. I know we can protect these babies. And we will, no matter what happens, but I need to be strong for that, and we all know that a pregnant shifter loses some of their own strength to care for their pups or cubs."

"Gavin and I, as well as everyone else in this Pack, would never let anything happen to you." My words were a growl and I hadn't even meant them to be. Audrey just smiled as Monday snuggled closer to me in her sleep, trying to comfort me.

"The babies want you to remember that it is okay. That we are making do."

"You say that, and yet I feel like I'm making another mistake."

"You aren't. Just breathe. It is okay. Now, I know you have a lot of work to do today. So why don't you just go do that, and I will take these sleeping babies back to their home."

"I'd rather sit here with the puppies."

At that, all three rolled up, their paws in the air, and yipped and barked. I couldn't help but laugh.

"Okay, it looks like they were playing along. Sneaky little puppies." They moved so that all of them were standing in my lap, their paws on my shoulders, and I growled low, nipping at their noses. They needed to learn dominance and who their Alpha was, so in case of an emergency and for their safety, they would listen without hesitation. And it would also keep their wolf happy. Wolves needed the hierarchy. Honestly, their humans did too. But it was more important for their animals to realize who was in charge and who would comfort them and keep them safe no matter what. That's why shifters needed a different kind of control than humans.

They all scrambled over my lap and towards Audrey, who waved and headed back to where the other children were and where the maternals could keep them safe and out of trouble. Or at least as out of trouble as possible.

I sighed and stood up, dusting the dirt off my pants.

"Alpha, can you come over for a minute?" Ronin asked, and I looked over at one of the newer wolves to our den. Ronin had been bitten over a year ago by a lone wolf and forced to change. Because of where the bite had been, he had nearly died, which was why he had been able to shift at all, instead of just healing like a human. He hadn't had a Pack for the first couple of months and that had hindered his control his wolf, but now, working with the soldiers and trainers, he was getting better. I liked the kid, and he was finally settling into his fur easier.

"How can I help, Ronin?"

Ronin didn't meet my gaze, since he was lower on the dominance scale and his wolf wouldn't allow him, but I reached out and squeezed his shoulder. He relaxed easily, and just like that, he was fine. He wasn't scared of my wolf. His wolf was just figuring out how to feel connected and loved. It was a balance, and all of us were working on it.

"We're trying to put up this new wall on the barn, and we could use your strength."

I blinked. "You need help with an actual barn raising?" I asked, smiling.

"Pretty much. What do you say?"

I laughed and followed him to the barn where they were indeed raising it like in the old days before mechanical equipment could make it easier.

"Is there a reason you're doing this, Seamus?" I asked.

The older wolf just shrugged. "I was feeling nostalgic. Now I regret it. But we need a barn for the sheep."

I laughed at that, the submissive wolf having been a farmer for longer than I had been alive. And yes, we did raise sheep for wool and had other animals on our land, too. We'd been forced to be self-sustaining for so long. We had a different society than many of the Packs did. Or, at least, how they did now. Everyone had been forced to rely solely on themselves. We had just been doing it for longer.

I helped them raise the barn, my muscles straining as we did so without pulleys or anything, just using our strength. But it's what we had done in the past and what Seamus had wanted us to do now. It was fun, and although I had to stay away from the actual sheep because they would cower in fear, Seamus and Ronin could walk through the flock as if they knew that they wouldn't hurt them.

It was an odd sight to see, and I wasn't sure that any other Pack had a flock, but we did. And we kept them safe.

"Well, it always makes me laugh when I see Seamus walking through the sheep like that."

I looked over at the familiar voice to find Malissa smiling up at me.

Her wolf was in her gaze, and it was hungry.

"That's what I was just thinking."

I didn't reach out and touch her, to pull her near me like I would any other wolf that didn't hate me. Wolves needed touch, comfort. They needed to know their Alpha was there for them. And yes, some of the wolves that didn't trust me wouldn't take kindly to me doing that, and Malissa used to be one of them. But now, she was bordering on the edge of not understanding why I didn't want to be with her. So I had to make sure I didn't lead her on.

"What are you doing for lunch? Can I take you out?"

"I promised the pups I'd eat with them later."

"Oh, that's okay. Maybe some other time. It's good to see you out and about though, Alpha. The Pack needs it."

I nodded, not sure if I agreed.

"Perhaps. I'm just doing my part. I had the strength." I gestured towards the barn. Malissa's gaze raked down my body and my wolf growled, not liking that.

"Well, I would say something, but I don't want to come on too strong."

I snorted. "What are you up to today, Malissa?"

"This and that. I'm going to go help Dara with a few things. She and Lily are working on some research, and I said I would pore through books."

I straightened, on alert. "Did they get the books from the coven then?"

Malissa nodded. "They did. I might not be a witch, but I can research. So I'm going to help them and Wynter, when she gets off work, to look through everything. We're going to try to find a way to work this magic. There has to be something."

"Do I want to know how Dara got the books?"

Malissa held up her hands. "I don't know. I didn't ask."

She reached forward, grazed her fingers down my arm. "I'll leave you then, Alpha. But call me when you need to take care of that wolf, okay? We don't want our Alpha to be too pent up."

And with that, she sauntered off. I just shook my head. I needed to be thinking about the magic that they were working on and not anything else. Because damn it, what the hell was wrong with me today?

I didn't feel anything towards Malissa, and if she had been using her nose, she would have realized that I wasn't wound-up tight because I had someone to release that tension.

And as if I had conjured her, the wind adjusted just right so her scent hit me straight on, my cock pressing hard against my zipper.

Skye stood there, a bag slung over her shoulder, her eyes narrowed.

She had seen the touch, and I didn't know what I felt about it because Skye wasn't mine. Just like I wasn't Skye's. But I also didn't have privileges with anyone else. I wasn't like that.

I opened my mouth to say something, but Skye spoke first as she came to my side. "I overheard part of that. Do you want me to call my aunt about the magic books?" she asked, as if she hadn't seen Malissa come on to me.

"I'm pretty sure Dara already did. We wouldn't work on this without you guys."

She nodded tightly, her gaze straight on my arm where Malissa had touched, and then she smiled up at me. "Well, I'm on my way to go see Audrey. I know she's with the pups today, but she promised me that she would help me with a few things."

"If you're sure. It's good to see you."

She smiled softly, and I didn't know how I felt about that, but it did twist me up inside. I wanted to reach out, to kiss her, to tell her I was sorry. But there was nothing to be sorry about. Because she wasn't my mate. And I wasn't hers.

"Stop looking at me like that. You're allowed to have other women flirt with you. You're not my mate. I know that."

I sighed, then finally gave in, brushing my fingers along her skin. Others were looking, but they already knew that we were sleeping together. It was hard to hide those scents. I just tried not to touch her in public because I didn't want her to be looked at with pity because she had been with the Alpha. Especially when this ended.

Her eyes went gold, her wolf in her gaze, and I felt like she knew where my thoughts had gone.

"I don't want to hurt your feelings or your wolf's. I'm not with anybody else, Skye."

She smiled softly and then went up to her tiptoes and kissed me, her lips a soft brush that soothed my wolf and my soul in one instant. How could she do that so easily?

"I know you aren't. You're not that kind of man. But I also know that one day you're going to find your mate, and I will walk away. That was the rule that we had. The rule that all wolves have when it comes to dalliances like this. It's okay, Chase. So someone finds you hot. Shocking. So do I."

My lips twitched, and I held out my hand. Her eyes widened, and yet she still took it, tangling her fingers with mine. "Come on. I'll walk you to Audrey."

"If you're sure."

"Skye. Let me do this. Okay?"

My heart twisted inside my chest, but she nodded. We walked together, and people stared at us, but didn't say anything. Some people looked on in awe, others in happiness. Others in curiosity or anger. Because I was their Alpha, and here I was, with a woman that wasn't my mate and not even Pack. But I was allowed this comfort. Wasn't I? I just couldn't hurt her.

And when the time came to walk away from her, it would break me. But it had to be the only option.

Because, in the end, while I didn't know how to break the magic of the vampire or how to earn my Pack's trust, I knew one thing.

Skye Anderson was not my mate.

And she never would be.

CHAPTER
TWELVE

Skye

"Mom. Seriously? I don't have time for this."

I scrunched my face as Cailin Jamenson Anderson wiped soot off of my chin and then went back to lick her thumb before trying to touch my face again.

"Ack. No. We're not doing this. I'm an adult. You don't get to spit on your hand and then touch me."

Mom just winked at me and then wiped her hands on her jeans. "I was just seeing how far you'd let me go. I love you, baby."

I blushed, I couldn't help it. It wasn't like we were in a hidden space where nobody could watch us. No,

151

we were outside the den boundaries, and I was about to head on patrol. My mother had just finished hers and was going in to train some of the teenagers who were getting a little antsy and bored. We constantly trained with each other and those below us, not just for war or battle, but because we needed to make sure our wolves knew that the humans needed to be in control. With teenage hormones going rampant, it was very important for us to ensure that the teenagers had full control and knowledge of their wolves as their strengths and magic fluctuated along with their bodies.

"Say hi to the babies for me."

"I'm working with the teens today. Your father's working with the toddlers."

That made me grin. Many toddlers could shift, since some learned how to shift when they were two or three, others younger. It all depended on the wolf and wasn't necessarily an indication of strength.

And because toddlers could shift into an animal, they needed to find peace with their other half so they didn't grow too aggressive or let their wolves too close to the surface.

Today, my father would be playing chase with little wolves as they learned not to use their claws while playing, and would be the cutest little things ever.

"I'm sad I'm going to be missing that."

"You're always welcome to come to visit and do toddler training with Dad."

"I just like that it's Dad doing it. He was always great with us."

"Yes, he was." Mom cupped my chin. "Be safe out there. I know you're an adult, like your brothers and cousins. All of you are strong and take no shit. But you're all still my babies, and there are vampires out there that want to hurt you. And rogues, and these hybrids, and humans that don't like who we are. For all we know, there's something else hidden around the corner."

"Mom. I'm okay. We work well together, remember?"

"I know. You are a brilliant wolf. And I love the woman that you've become. The place you've taken in this Pack as someone who can always be counted on."

My eyes stung and I swallowed hard. It was odd for me to even react to that because I didn't feel like I always fit in. I was Redwood. I would always be Redwood, even if I somehow found my mate in another Pack or found my position in another Pack. My soul would always be connected to the Redwoods. But I didn't have a title like some of my cousins. I didn't have a position in the Pack beyond soldier or runner. I fit in wherever they needed me to, and nowhere all at the same time. My mother seemed to understand what was going on in my mind, and she leaned forward and kissed both cheeks, then my forehead.

"Be safe. And I will see you when you get back. You are always part of this Pack, and my heart. Know that, Skye. Patricia." Her voice broke as she said the word, and I smiled softly before I let her walk away. I always wondered why she had named me after her mother, and my brother after her father. Because, in the end, while my brother went by Edward, I did not go by Patricia. I didn't like how much it hurt my mom to think of the woman who sacrificed herself to save my father. To save our Pack. So I went by Skye.

I didn't know what I would do if I ever lost my mother.

"You ready to go?" Adalyn asked, and I turned to see my friend and fellow patrol member for the day. We were scouring the neutral zone today since the council had just finished their meeting, and we didn't know if the vampires would come again. Each of the Packs had sent members for this certain patrol. It was a new joint task that we were trying, and if it meant I got to run with Adalyn, I was happy. I liked her.

Of course, my wolf scented another person that had come and I tried not to groan.

And from the way that Adalyn's shoulders tensed, she saw the other person who had joined him.

"Two Alphas on patrol? That's not asking for trouble," I grumbled as I looked toward Chase and Cole.

Adalyn let out a breath. "They need to show that they're not going to be hiding within the wards. And it gives everybody else a boost in morale to see them running and protecting the Pack. It's not all behind closed doors."

"True. It makes us a little grumbly."

Adalyn's brows lifted. "Maybe you just want to go over there and jump his bones. That might boost morale."

I shoved at her playfully. "Enough of that. Let's go do this shift, and try not to grumble."

"We'll see how long that lasts," she teased.

We made our way to get our orders, and I tried not to look in Chase's direction for too long. My wolf wanted to press against him, just to feel him. But there was no tug on the mating bond. No mating urge for Chase.

He wasn't mine.

And yet, what if he could be?

I quickly pushed those thoughts from my mind. That would not help anybody right then.

But I wanted it to. So badly.

And that was my own downfall.

Chase gave me a look and I swallowed hard, trying to focus on my breathing. What the hell was wrong with me? I was stronger than this. I needed to be stronger than this. I didn't need to get all cow-eyed over a boy.

But Chase was no boy. He was an Alpha. And I needed to remember that.

"Now that we're all here, Cole, Frederick, Gaston, and James will take one path. The rest will follow me," Chase said as my wolf pushed at me.

"Do you want us in wolf form or human form?" I asked, trying not to let my wolf be in control. I needed to be stronger than this. Just because Chase wasn't touching me just then didn't mean he wouldn't touch me again. We were working, for goddess's sake.

"Human form's fine unless you prefer to be in wolf form. Either way, let's get going. We have the whole territory on this side to work through, which means we're going to end up on Aspen Pack land by the end of it."

I nodded tightly, swallowed hard, and tried to get myself under control. Just because I was losing my mind didn't mean everyone else had to see that.

We followed along the route that we had discussed, not necessarily running but going at a brisk pace. I kept my senses on alert, ready to protect my Pack no matter what happened. I just didn't like that we didn't know when these vampires were going to come for us.

"Is something wrong?" Chase asked as I looked over at him. I shook my head.

My wolf pushed at me, wanting me to be honest, while the human part of me wanted no part of that. "No. I'm fine. I am just thinking."

"You don't have to stay away from me. Everyone knows we're together, Skye. You don't have to shy away from me unless you want to."

I looked at him then and laughed softly. "I'm being weird, aren't I?"

"No, it's not just you. I'm sorry. I hate acting weird."

Still moving, others around us spread through the area, people discussing their theories on the vampires or even what they were doing after this patrol. Chase and I were paired off, just like everybody else was, and I swallowed hard.

He stopped then, and I did too, and when he leaned forward, brushing his knuckles against my cheek, my wolf calmed.

Damn him, my wolf calmed. I did not want my wolf to calm in this position. Because that meant my wolf wanted to need him. And I couldn't want to need him.

"I needed to touch you. I hope that's okay?"

"More than okay," I whispered, the words leaving me before I thought better of it.

"We're not handling this whole working together thing well, are we?" he asked, his voice a rough chuckle.

"We aren't. Because I don't usually go on patrol with the men that I sleep with."

And that was true. I didn't tend to do that. Honestly, I dated humans outside of the den more than wolves, mainly because that's how it worked out. It didn't help that sometimes I felt like I was related to three-quarters of the Redwood Pack. It wasn't the case, but I couldn't help that thought.

I was past my majority, a full adult in the Redwood Pack, yet I still felt like a little kid sometimes.

Chase wasn't the first wolf I'd been with, and I had to remind myself that he wouldn't be the last because this wasn't forever.

"I need to protect my people," Chase whispered, and I nodded tightly, disappointment sliding through me even though it didn't make any sense.

"So do I. So, I'm going to shift into wolf form. I'll be as quick as possible, though."

Chase smiled at me and nodded before he moved back, giving me space.

The change was agony and ecstasy, pain and bliss all rolled into one. Bones broke, tendons tore, muscles reshaped. I was wolf, howling as one, two souls merged. I was as quick as possible, grateful that I could still be on alert while I changed. Chase had my back, and honestly, one of us should be in our wolf form anyway. It was easier to fight that way, although it did mean I couldn't communicate with him. Perhaps that was a good thing.

I trotted with him, grateful that he had stuck my

clothes in the pack that I had been holding, and now carried it for me. It was nice to know that I wasn't alone. Of course, in this form, he scented even stronger of man and thunderstorms and forest. Everything that my wolf craved, but I was stronger than this. I moved, keeping on alert.

When another Pack member asked him for something, I moved away, partnering with another Central member I didn't know well. A few of us had shifted to wolf form, needing the wind in our fur and the dirt beneath our paws. I could sense them all around, knowing that we were here for a purpose, protecting those we cared about, and being alert because vampires had been scented here earlier that day. Vampires we could not find.

And then another Pack member needed Chase, and then someone else, and another. The closer we got to the Aspen Pack den, the more people who needed his time, the more people who gave me odd looks, wondering what I would do.

I told myself I was reading far too much into the looks. It wasn't as if I were Chase's girlfriend or mate. I was just...here. For now.

It didn't matter because I was Redwood, and Chase was mine only for a moment. I knew people were wondering exactly what was going on between us. The fact that the two of us didn't know either just meant that it was our issue. Nobody else needed to understand our business. It wasn't like I knew what our business was.

I wasn't in the mood for people to keep giving me odd looks as if wondering how I was the one with the Aspen Pack Alpha.

Of course, Malissa was there on patrol, close to Chase, as if I hadn't been with him the night before. And though Chase and I were both being monogamous with each other, I saw the connection between the two.

I couldn't help but see it.

The way that his wolf moved towards her as if it sensed something he didn't sense in me.

Maybe it was just an Alpha soothing a Packmate, or maybe it was something more.

I didn't like this jealousy within me. He wasn't mine, not really. And I needed to be careful. Oh, so careful.

We kept moving, the others speaking around us as we traded shifts with another team and moved to another set of patrols along the perimeter. This was my evening, keeping on alert and trying not to be so far in my head.

Because I was cognizant of that, I heard the first branch break and stilled. Adalyn was by my side then, and she muttered under her breath.

"I can scent them too."

The first vampire strolled out of the woods as if he

hadn't a care in the world. This was one of the vampires with full knowledge of what he was doing. He wasn't a rogue. And as he cast out a scent lure, I cursed, grateful I was in my wolf form.

Adalyn took one step forward, the lure wrapping around her as if the scent was intoxicating and too much.

I pressed myself in between her and the vampire, and she shook herself out of her reverie.

"What the fuck was that?" Her words were a growl, and I knew we'd have to tell the others about the strength of the lure later. We didn't have time right then, however.

I growled low, baring fangs, and another vampire came out of the forest, and then another, and then there were twenty.

The wolves rang out the alarm, and I pounced, the nearest vampire baring fangs, growling as if he owned this land and we were the interlopers.

The vampire tossed out his scent again, and Adalyn fell to her knees, screaming.

Black magic pulsated in the air, the black dust from before burning flesh, but I ducked underneath the mass, my paws slamming into the ground as I moved, my claws raking into the dirt. And when I jumped, I bit the vampire on the arm. It dropped the bag of magic it held and sliced out, but not using its talons.

I let out an angry and hurt-filled yelp, hitting the ground on my side as its blade dug into my chest. I scrambled, trying to get up, but it slashed at me, claw after claw, the black magic dust seeping into my pores. I roared, and then Adalyn was there, slicing the vampire's head off. Others were moving toward me as blood seeped from my side, and I tried to move, tried to shift back, tried to do anything, but I didn't have control of anything. All I could do was heave out my breath, trying to figure out what to do next. Then Adalyn was there, her hands on my side, her eyes wide.

"Oh my God. It stopped me. It wouldn't let me move. We're going to get you help. We'll get your Healer. Stay with me, Skye."

There was a roar, an anguished echo that wasn't from Adalyn or myself or any one of the Redwoods. No, that was Chase. He roared, pummeling through the vampires, his angry gaze set on me.

It was as if he blamed me for getting stabbed by something I didn't understand.

I cursed myself, and then the shift began again, not of my own making. I scrambled, little yips escaping my throat as suddenly I was human, shifting far too fast, far faster than I had ever done in my life. Blood soaked me as the knife stayed embedded in my ribcage below my heart. The dagger had missed my vital organs, but just barely.

I choked on blood, the black dust magic seeping into my pores, and I tried to rub it off, my eyes wide. I didn't care that I was naked, that others were shouting and fighting around me.

"Adalyn," I choked, my mouth filled with blood.

"I need to move the dagger. I don't know what's wrong with it. It's doing something to your wolf."

The panic the other woman tried to hide echoed within my own thoughts.

"Don't!" Wren shouted as she came towards us, Dara by her side.

"It's coated with magic," the harvester witch said as both she and the Healer knelt by my side. "I'm going to have to use a chant to stop it. It's why you shifted back. Your wolf was repelled by it. I'll help, don't worry."

"I'm not your Healer, but I am a doctor. I've gone through medical school. I will help you. And your Healer will get here soon. You will be fine, Skye."

I looked up at them, trying to reach my wolf and find the bond to that other soul, but there was nothing.

I looked up at them, pain filling me, and then Chase was there, kneeling by my head.

"You'll be fine, Skye. Breathe. Nothing's going to hurt you."

"The vampires?" I asked as the others worked on me, and I tried to ignore the fiery pain in my side.

"Go," Adalyn barked at her Alpha, her eyes downcast. It only occurred to me then that I was meeting Chase's eyes, but nobody else was.

"Don't order me around, Adalyn."

She shuddered under his magic, and I cursed.

"Chase," I rasped. "They need you."

"Skye."

I looked at him then, angry. And I wasn't sure what I was supposed to say. I wasn't sure if there was anything to say.

"I'm Redwood. The Aspens need you."

"You got fucking hurt."

The others were abnormally quiet, and I knew it was because they were all scared. Hell, I was terrified by the way he was acting. He was not my mate, and yet he was surely acting like it. He didn't get that choice, though. He wasn't mine.

"You're not my Alpha. The others need you. Stop trying to protect me. I'm Redwood."

The silence was so loud at that moment that I could barely breathe.

"You are, aren't you?" He glared at the others. "Protect her."

"We are, Alpha," Wren whispered.

"Don't get fucking hurt again," he snarled at me. And with that, he stormed off. Moments later, I felt the magic slide out of me, Dara's spell working through my bones.

"Well, that was interesting," Adalyn murmured as Wren worked.

"The spell seemed to have healed you too," Wren added, ignoring what had just happened with Chase. I didn't know if anyone else was going to.

I looked up at her, noticing then that the pain was weakening.

Wren gave me a small smile, her eyes kind. "We'll get your Healer here. You'll be okay. Despite what our Alpha is growling about."

I shook my head, angry with myself. Because Chase was growling like I was his. But he wasn't. I wasn't his, and he wasn't mine. I needed my Pack. I needed my family.

I didn't need to be here with him.

And I didn't want to keep making mistake after mistake. Getting hurt as badly as I had, letting the magic hit me as it had because I hadn't been paying attention. If I'd been doing my job, maybe I would've been better off.

I didn't know what I could do, but I couldn't be with Chase. Not if I wanted to remain sane.

Not if I wanted to keep myself somewhat whole.

THIRTEEN

Skye

"THANK YOU FOR SAVING ME FROM MY MOTHER," I said on a laugh, ignoring the twinge in my side.

Both Audrey and Adalyn just shook their heads, Audrey's lips twitching.

"I'll be sure not to tell your mother that."

"Oh, I think I will. Or maybe I'll tell that cousin of yours, and then he can tease you." Adalyn beamed, and while I might have enough cousins to fill a football stadium, I knew exactly which one she spoke of.

"You do that, and I will tell Nico your weaknesses."

The hunter narrowed her gaze at me, even as her lips twitched. "You aren't playing fair."

"You're the one who wants to give me up to him. I'm just saying."

"This is nice, this girl time with us." I looked over as Dara spoke, the witch rubbing the back of her neck as she put her feet up on the couch.

My mother had been taking most of the past week to pamper me, to the point that I was exhausted. I was nearly fully healed from the attack. That poison and that magic-covered blade had done its damage. But as soon as the magic had dissipated, the wound itself healed mostly on its own. I hadn't needed my own Healer, since the Aspen Pack Healer had tried to help as much as possible.

No, even though I'd had a dagger in my side, the magic was what had done the most damage. Magic we were all a little worried about, considering there were no cures or ways to fight it that we knew of.

After a week of my mother's attention, trying to baby me even in my own home, Adalyn and Audrey had kidnapped me. I was grateful and fully healed. I didn't need to have my mother worrying about me as if I was a child that needed saving over and over again.

We were now at Adalyn's house, Audrey having decided that she needed a girls' night as well, so Gavin went out with the guys.

Dara was here, as were Wren and Wynter, and Novah. Lily was out on another date, and I could not wait to meet this man who made the woman smile.

It was odd to think that I was enjoying my girl time with the Aspens so much. It hadn't even occurred to me to try to find girl time with my friends back in the Redwoods. Because I was friends with them, but honestly, they were family more than just friends. These women didn't think of me as the Redwood Pack princess. Instead, they thought of me as their friend, one who fought with them, the one who constantly threw herself in front of Chase to save his life, and possibly something more.

"I'm sad that Lily isn't here to join us. I want to know more about this man of hers," Novah said as she leaned back into her chair and began to knit. Novah and Audrey were the only two mated women in our group. I didn't know Novah that well, other than she was a Truth Seeker. That meant, if she used her magic, she could find the truth of someone's words and tell if they were lying. Novah had promised that she wasn't going to use her magic consciously with us, and I was grateful. Because if we were talking about Lily and her guy, the conversation might just end up going back to Chase, and that wasn't something I was ready for.

"None of us know who he is, and I think she likes

having something just for herself, you know?" Wynter added, smiling softly.

Wynter was a human member of the Pack, which wasn't unheard of, but still pretty rare. She wasn't mated in, and I didn't know her story, but it was still nice to get to know her. She worked in the city, outside the den, but had a small home on Pack land. She was also training with Adalyn and was a decent shot.

It made me sad to think that everybody within a Pack had to learn how to protect themselves, and it wasn't "just in case." No, they needed to do so in order to protect their den and our children.

"We'll get it out of her soon," Wren said softly as she smiled at all of us. She was gorgeous. Her light-blond hair was pulled back in an intricate braid. She was a lynx, the only lynx that I knew, and I loved when she was in her cat form. She was sturdy and compact and adorable. Not that I would ever tell her that. No, she might be slightly submissive and a Healer, but she could probably kick my ass.

"Well, since we're discussing dates," Audrey said as she fluttered her eyelashes.

I threw a piece of popcorn at her. "Let's not."

"Oh, let's," Wynter said as she clapped her hands. "I've been working so much recently I don't know the whole scoop."

"Yes, I would like to know the scoop too," Novah

put in.

I narrowed my eyes at the Truth Seeker. "Oh no, you don't. Don't use your wicked magic on me."

Novah laughed, putting her hands over her heart as if she were innocent. "I would never."

"You know, I don't believe her," Dara said, her eyes filled with laughter. It was good, because Dara rarely smiled these days since she was so exhausted fending off the vampire magic. I knew that Lily and some of the other witches around were helping, but Dara was the strongest here, and it was too much for her alone.

"I'm not saying a thing."

"You know that just makes me want to know more," Adalyn added.

I sighed. "There's nothing. I don't even know if we'll see each other again. I sort of growled at him, and he did the same to me."

"Because you keep getting hurt trying to save him." Audrey shook her head. "He might be Alpha, and it's our job to protect him, but he's still a dominant wolf, and his job is to protect us at the same time. He doesn't like that you're hurt."

I looked down at my hands and let out a breath, my wolf tugging at the bond between us. "He's not my mate. We know that. So I don't know why he's being so possessive. He yelled at me, and he's not my Alpha."

"I know he's not your Alpha, but he *is* one. And who

says you're not mates? It could happen." Audrey came forward and squeezed my hand. "I, above all people, know it can happen."

I wanted to cry right then, and I didn't know why. My wolf paced as emotions raced through me. "He's not. We've been very clear on that. We're just comforting each other while waiting for our mates to show up with little bows on them." I rolled my eyes. "It sounds stupid when I say it out loud."

"It's not stupid," Wren put in. "If we were only ever with our mate, waiting centuries for them to show up, it would be a very lonely existence. And our animals need touch. They need that friendship that comes from being with one another."

"As the only human here, I can tell you the same thing. Humans date all the time, and so do witches."

"Hear, hear!" Dara put in.

"And I'm a latent wolf, and before I was mated to Cassius, I had men that I was with. It's okay for you to be with someone knowing that it's not a soulmate attachment for forever." Novah paused. "You can love someone, even if they aren't your mate."

I held up my hands, my pulse racing. "Whoa, whoa, whoa. Nobody said anything about love."

"I didn't think we had to," Audrey said softly.

I shook my head and set down my popcorn. "I don't think so. I don't love him. Yes, I have some weird feelings for him, and that's just because it's complicated. I have my own issues within my Pack, about hierarchy and all of that, in addition to the fact that these vampires are attacking us, and we don't know how to stop them. They're hurting us, and we can't get a foot on the ground. So yes, everything's complicated, but I am not in love with him."

The girls looked at each other, and I wanted to hide under my blanket. I didn't, but only barely.

Wren leaned forward. "So he's not your mate. But you are friends. And he yelled at you in front of everybody. I mean, that wasn't very nice."

"Because he doesn't like the fact that I get hurt protecting him. But he gets hurt protecting all of us. I'm the weak one who keeps getting stabbed or shot with magic. And somebody is out there trying to hurt Chase. Somebody is trying to slice magic into him, or find him, or do something to him. He's the center of this, so therefore we all have to be on high alert to protect him."

Everyone started talking at once, agreeing with me. Because they were after Chase, and just because I was the one that constantly put myself on the line, it didn't mean that Chase needed to protect me.

"We're going to go back to that whole hierarchy thing," Adalyn whispered. "Because you are fierce and strong. And there's just something about you, Skye. There's nothing weak about you."

I looked at the other woman, at the dominant wolf who should have been higher in the hierarchy than she was, but the moon goddess hadn't blessed her. What was it about us? What pulled us away from our potential?

Before I could ask that though, the door opened, and a woman with strawberry blond hair and a bright smile walked in. I tried to ignore the resentment, the way that my wolf stood up, her tail bushy at the sight of Malissa.

Malissa just waved. "I'm sorry I'm late. But I brought cheesecake."

Audrey grinned, stood up, hugged the other woman tight, and took the cheesecake from her. "I know you were working, so cheesecake makes me happy."

"I love cheesecake, thank you," I said, trying to sound civil.

I saw Adalyn fighting a smile, but no one else seemed to notice. Of course, I wasn't looking at Novah for a reason. I didn't want to know what the Truth Seeker saw.

"It's a cheesecake with strawberries and whipped cream. My favorite. I had to work late, but I did come bearing dessert, so I hope that counts."

Malissa took the seat next to me and my wolf bristled, but hopefully nobody else noticed. She had a thing for the Alpha, but I didn't have any claim to him.

Malissa handed me a slice of cheesecake, and I

smiled at the other woman, trying not to feel resentful that she and Chase seemed to have a connection that I didn't understand. Perhaps it was just that he was Alpha, and she was a slightly submissive wolf and needed that dominant wolf. Or it was the fact that I felt, in my heart of hearts, like perhaps they could be mates. I saw the way that Chase looked at her as if trying to piece together what it was about her.

There was something wrong with me. And I hated it.

Malissa leaned close to me, my wolf freezing. "By the way, I just wanted to let you know that I'm sorry for trying to poach."

I nearly dropped my cheesecake and looked at the other woman. "What?"

She blushed, ducking her head. "I hadn't realized that you and Chase were in a relationship when I asked him out. I feel like an idiot. But nobody told me, and I didn't catch the signs because I sometimes get lost in my head like an idiot but don't worry, he is all yours. I promise not to be an idiot again."

"Oh, well, he's not, well, oh."

I was mumbling, but she just smiled and moved into conversation with Dara, as if she hadn't just rocked my world off its axis again.

That was the thing with wolves, though. As Malissa said, we understood our territories and connections, and we didn't poach. Only, Chase wasn't mine. We had been very firm on that, even if we kept acting like that wasn't true.

"I need to head out," Novah said, after another hour of food and laughter and drinks. "I promised my mate I'd be home for date night." She grinned as everybody whistled, but she just shrugged. "I can't help it. I can't wait to make sure I mark him again. I may be latent, but I'm possessive."

I wiped the crumbs off my lap and stood up, grateful that my side no longer twinged. "While I could stay for most of the day, I do believe my mother will have a fit if I'm gone for too long."

"Yes, it's not like you're an adult or anything," Wynter said with a laugh, and I shrugged.

"I just do what my mother says. Like a good daughter."

They all burst out laughing at that, knowing it for the lie it was. We said our goodbyes, and I was grateful for this connection, these feelings. These were my friends. They might not be Pack, but they felt like something just as good.

Connections I wouldn't have without visiting the Aspens as much as I did.

"You're welcome to stay here if you'd like," Adalyn said as we all finished cleaning up.

"No, I need to go home. I appreciate all of you,

though. Seriously." I hugged Adalyn hard, then the others, and followed Novah out the door, knowing that the others would follow suit soon.

"I'm glad that you came tonight. I know that you are technically a Redwood, but in my heart, you're also a little bit Aspen."

I blinked. "Really? That's nice." My wolf didn't know what to think about the words, however, since we were Redwood.

"With the way our four Packs are integrating and mingling these days, sometimes it doesn't feel like they're separate anymore." She let out a long breath. "After everything that we went through before, it's nice to see my family finding their center again."

"I get that. I wasn't alive during the war when we almost lost my Pack the first time, but I understand the ramifications of all of it."

Novah met my gaze, and I had a feeling she was using her powers, even if she didn't mean to. They were part of her. So hindering them didn't always work. "You know, I do believe you understand exactly."

I cleared my throat, only slightly unnerved at the way I knew she saw the truth. "I have a bit of a drive to get home, so thank you for walking me this far."

"Well, I may have led you astray. I can't help it." She winked, and before I could ask what she meant, a familiar scent hit my nostrils and I held back a curse.

It seemed everybody was trying to get in the middle of these things. Novah went off towards Cassius as the man standing next to him glared at me.

Yes, glared. As if I had done something wrong.

"Behave, Alpha," Novah said as she tapped him on the nose after going to her tiptoes. I couldn't believe her audacity, but as Cassius pulled her away, I was grateful for it.

"You're going home alone?" Chase asked in lieu of greeting.

"I'm an adult, so yes."

"Should still be on bedrest."

We were alone on the path, so I just shook my head. "I don't need to be. It's been a week, Chase. I'm fine. All healed up."

"I'll be the judge of that."

"No, you won't. My Healer was the judge of that. And I know my own body. You don't need to worry about me constantly, Chase." I let out a breath, my wolf yearning and angry all at the same time. "You don't need to yell at me like I'm one of yours."

"You protect me as if you're one of mine. So I should be able to yell at you." He cupped my face then, something that I had wanted him to do from the first. "I don't like you hurt. We could have lost you."

I shook my head. "But you didn't lose me. That's the whole point."

"I want to check your wound myself."

I looked up at him then, a smile spreading on my face. "Was that a line?"

A blush covered his cheekbones, just a slash of pink before it dissipated quickly. "It wasn't, but now that you say it..." his voice trailed off.

I swallowed hard. "Well then, Chase. You surprise me."

"I don't want to surprise you. Not this time. I just need to make sure you're safe."

I looked up at him, trailing my fingers down his cheekbone. "What are we doing?" I asked, and not for the first time.

"We're friends. And friends make sure the others aren't hurt."

"I can do that."

And knowing I was making a mistake, I slid my hand into his and followed him to his place. I quickly shot off a text to my mother saying I would be late, but I didn't tell her why. I was an adult, and though she was worried about my health and my safety, that didn't mean she got to know precisely where I was at all times. Or who I was with.

I had tried to stay away from Chase. But I wasn't going to succeed because everybody was right. I was allowed to take comfort for now and to have a little hope. Every time I turned around, we were being attacked or finding magic that we didn't understand. I needed this. And so, when Chase slowly stripped me from my clothes, checking the wound at my side, the scar I would forever have because of the magic that inflicted it, I let him touch me. And I let him kiss me. And I kissed him back. And I pulled his shirt off, kissing over his chest, exactly where he had almost been killed in battle before. And over the scars that I hadn't asked about, the ones that had come from a cage, the ones that I hoped one day he would tell me about.

He set his hands over my breasts, sucking and kissing me softly, and then we were on his bed, an Alpha's bed, and I felt like this was home. This was everything.

"You're so beautiful," he whispered, and I swallowed hard, as he continued to hold me, to kiss me.

"You're not so bad looking yourself," I whispered, and then he nipped my lip.

I had been so angry before, just like he had been. We were supposed to be angry. Upset about the attack and healing, and yet all I could do was run my hands over him, to strip him completely bare just as he had done me. He lowered himself, pressing my thighs to the bed so he could lick and suck on my pussy. I swallowed hard, running my hands over my breasts, my nipples, as he continued to kiss me, continued to play with me.

I came with a gasp, his lips on my clit, before I

moved, pressing him down into the bed and taking him into my mouth. He groaned, tugging at my hair, but I kept moving, sucking him, needing him. I slid my hands over his balls, around his length, just needing to taste him, to be in control for just one moment because I was never in control when it came to him.

He was an Alpha. I wasn't even supposed to meet his gaze, and here I was, hovering above him.

When he was about to come, he tugged on my head harder. I pulled away and went on all fours, letting him slide deep into me with one quick thrust. I clamped down around him, my body shaking, and he moved, pummeling into me as both of us breathed as one, my hands digging into the comforter as he bit down on my shoulder, not breaking the skin, not marking me as his. But he was losing control, just like I was. His hands were over my breasts, over my sides, and when they dipped between my cheeks, slowly probing my other entrance, I tensed but let him play, sending me over the edge with just one finger, the movement swift, achingly tight, and pleasurable all at once. He slammed into me, over and over again. Just before he came he moved us, so I was on my back, him over me, his mouth crushed to mine. He filled me, my body shaking, and I wrapped myself around him, needing him.

After we cleaned up, I laid in his arms, neither one

of us bothering to speak as we fought to catch our breath.

"Well," I said after a moment. "I suppose we figured out if I'm healed or not."

He chuckled roughly and I felt it beneath my ear. "I suppose we figured that out."

I slid my hand through his hair, ignoring the way I shook. "I'm okay, Chase. Yes, it hurt. Yes, I'm pissed that they keep using these personal wards and magics that we don't understand. But we're using more than our witches, even if we don't have the coven. We can figure it out."

He let out a rough sigh that seemed to carry the weight of the world. "I know we will. I'm meeting with the other Alphas, we're going to bring all of our witches in, even those in Texas and England. We're going to find out how to break this magic and figure out how the vampires are using their demon origins to come at us. We need to stop reacting and be proactive. I don't want my people hurt. I don't want you hurt."

He squeezed my shoulder, and I sank into him, wondering why this felt different. Because we weren't just sleeping with one another now. No, he was talking to me about problems as an Alpha. Talking to me about the war. Why did everything feel different?

"I hate the fact that I can't protect my people all the

time. That no matter what I do, sometimes I'm the one watching you fall. I don't want that, Skye."

I was worried all over again, because this wasn't a discussion for me.

No, this was a discussion for an Alpha's mate.

"Chase, we all fight for you and each other. Nobody resents you for fighting alongside them. Nobody resents you for not being able to figure out exactly what these vampires are doing. We don't know everything, but we know more than we did before. And we'll continue to know more. You're a good Alpha, Chase. Believe in that."

He looked at me, a small smile on his face, and I had to wonder what he was thinking. Because he wouldn't tell me, and that was the problem.

"Not everybody believes in me, Skye. But you do. And I'll take that. Thank you." He kissed me again, as if he realized that we had both crossed the line that was going to be hard to step back from. Instead, I let him slide deep inside of me, and I let my mind go away, just into this moment, of him deep within me, of this being sex, not love, not anything.

It was what I needed.

It was the only way to survive.

And maybe, if I kept saying it, I would believe it.

CHAPTER
FOURTEEN

Chase

"DO YOU THINK YOU'RE JUST GOING TO GET OUT OF here, and everybody will accept you like before? Because they won't. Honestly, they didn't before this. Who do you think you are? Not my son."

Blade slashed out, the whip slicing into my skin as it had a thousand times before. The whip, the blades, the knives. Everything had slashed into my skin multiple times. The pain intensified, adding to the scars that would never heal. A wolf was supposed to be able to recover. To find a way through the darkness. But not me. Not with the silver and magic-inhibiting cage surrounding me. Blade only let me out of the cage once a day for whatever ministrations he had planned. The cell was too small. I couldn't stand up, couldn't roll and stretch. All I could do was pretend. Again. Just pretend.

"I'll find her. Just like I found you. Your mother wasn't safe. You're not safe. I'll find that little girl. And make sure she understands that you are worthless. She's not your mate. Because you know that, don't you? You know that no matter what happens, you will never find that mate of yours. I will never allow it. You can have this trash for the time being, and then I will see what else I give you. See what I do to her." He slammed the whip down, the slice into my skin a fiery pain that tore a scream from my mouth. I woke up with a start as Skye ran her hands down my arms, my chest.

"Chase. Wake up. Please. You have to wake up."

She slid her hands up and down my arms, keeping me close. "Chase. You're safe. You're awake. It's okay."

"What? Skye? What are you doing here?"

Panic hit me like an anvil and I pushed her down to the bed, hovering over her as I looked around, waiting for danger. "We have to get you out of here. Blade's going to find you. We can't let him find you."

Her eyes went wet, understanding filling them, as I finally clicked to what was happening.

Shame coated my tongue, and I pulled away. "Did I hurt you?"

"No. Chase. Are you okay?" She sat up and cupped my face. "Chase."

My wolf whimpered, and I felt as if I'd never been Alpha at that moment. An Alpha didn't lean. He was the one who others leaned on. "Don't. Don't look at me like that. I could have hurt you."

"But you didn't. You were protecting me. You know that. Do you want to talk about it?" she asked, her voice low.

I shook my head and stood up, realizing that we were both naked, the darkness settling around us, and I couldn't breathe.

I scrambled off the bed, wiped the sweat off my face, and headed toward my bathroom.

My house was the Alpha's house, not the one I had grown up in. Blade had never stepped foot onto this property. No, instead, when I became Alpha, and we had started taking better care of the Pack, I'd needed somewhere to live but hadn't wanted anything to do with Blade. Not only for myself and my own selfish reasons, but because I didn't want the others to look at me and see Blade. Even though that seemed like something that would happen until the end of my days, no matter what.

I had taken one of the empty homes and made it my own. It was a three-bedroom place, something that one day could be filled with a family. Though I didn't think it would ever be my own, not with what I knew of what faced me.

But others could visit, and they did. My team and hierarchy were often here, and Audrey would have children one day, the same with Novah. Pups and cubs would be within these walls, bringing joy.

And not just the pain of my own nightmares.

Wordlessly I turned on the shower and let the hot water scald me. Over my scars, over the pain that still ebbed and flowed within my body.

I could remember Blade, everything he had ever said to me. That was never going to fade away. No matter how many centuries I lived, I would still remember everything that my father said to me.

Everything that Blade did to me.

I wasn't sure I could ever tell the others what Blade had done. Yes, they could guess some, and Audrey had even seen some. So had Steele and the others who had been on the right side of history when Blade had gone maniacal.

But none of them had seen everything.

I didn't want to tell Skye what happened. I couldn't.

Because while my friends hadn't witnessed my captivity in full, the Foreseer had. The one who had been lost in eons past thanks to Blade's own magic and pain. Most had forgotten she had been part of the Pack for mere moments before she'd been whisked away to Blade's power.

But I remembered her.

AND THE WORDS THAT SHE SAID STILL BROKE ME TO this day.

"The water's too hot, Chase. You're going to scald your skin."

Skye was behind me, her breasts pressed to my back, not in a sensual way, but in the comforting way of Pack.

But she wasn't Pack. I couldn't feel her along with the bonds of Alpha.

Kade would be able to, as would any of the Redwoods. But I couldn't feel Skye.

When she had gotten hurt, Wren hadn't been able to use her Healing powers in the way she would have if Skye was Pack. When the emotions were too much and Skye was bouncing along the walls, Hayes couldn't use his Omega connections to soothe her.

Nobody could do anything for her on these den grounds, and yet she was here protecting us. Being with us.

I wasn't sure what I was supposed to do about that, or if there was anything I should do.

Because I wanted Skye here.

Only, I couldn't have her here.

"I'm fine," I lied.

She wrapped her arms around me, her wolf pressed against mine, and it was all I could do not to press her against the shower wall and sink into her heat, letting that soothe me even though I knew it would just take us one step closer to an absolution that would never come.

"I'm sorry I woke you."

I changed the temperature of the water, not for myself, but I didn't want Skye to be burned. If I could do anything right then, I could at least protect her. It wasn't like I had been doing a bang-up job of it before now.

"I wasn't sleeping that deeply anyway."

I turned, letting the water pound into my back as I ran my hands over her hair. Water slicked between us, and she looked up at me, her wolf in her gaze, curious.

"Why weren't you sleeping?"

"I was just thinking about everything that's happened in the past few weeks. It's been a lot. To say the least."

"It has. I've been focused on the Pack, keeping more people safe, and finding answers to questions I don't know yet. I feel like I'm not doing a good enough job of making sure you are okay."

She looked at me then and snorted, the laugh delicate.

"What did I say?"

"You, thinking that you're not paying enough attention. All you do is make sure that all of us are well and as healthy as we could possibly be. You never take time for yourself. Except for right now in the shower, and here I am, encroaching on your space and making sure that you're okay. You're a good Alpha, Chase."

"But not your Alpha," I whispered.

Skye looked at me then, sighed, and reached for the body wash. She poured it onto a loofah and then began to wash my chest, my shoulders. I took it from her and began to wash her as well, the act sensual and the heat pulsing between us, but we didn't go any further than that. Just cleaning each other off after my nightmare and the evening before.

"When I yelled at you that you weren't my Alpha, it was because I was angry. Angry and hurt. And embarrassed that I was hurt. I'm constantly the one bleeding and injured because I'm not strong enough." She rolled her eyes as she said it, both of us moving to rinse off. I frowned, turning off the water once we were clean, and reaching for a towel.

"I don't like the way that you say that."

"It's the truth. So, I'm not quite sure what you mean."

I toweled her off, being gentle on her skin because I wasn't sure she really let anyone else be gentle with her.

She was forever trying to prove herself, and I had to wonder what else I was missing.

"You might not be a typical dominant, but you're a fighter, skilled and constantly learning. You were everywhere that you needed, forever looking for places that you can help others. I'm not quite sure why you keep thinking that you're weak or something. And that's why you keep getting hurt."

"I don't have a position in the Pack, Chase." She shook her head and began to dress in soft pants and a top, the clothes she had been wearing the day prior. I changed into sweats and a t-shirt myself, glaring at her.

"You get hurt because you throw yourself in front of every obstacle, protecting those around you. You may not have a full position in the hierarchy, but a soldier is there to aid." And then I acknowledged the elephant in the room, the one thing I didn't understand either.

"You can meet my gaze, Skye. You can meet any dominant's gaze, and you don't back down. Why is that?"

She shook her head.

"I don't know. I'm broken."

She whispered the words, and I cursed under my breath, moving to cup her face.

"You aren't broken. Believe me. You are not broken, Skye. There is a strength in you that others don't understand. Maybe there's a reason that you don't fit in with other parts of the Redwood Pack. That you are still looking for that right position. Because you can meet another's gaze, but you're not a maternal. Not an Alpha."

"Then what am I?" she asked, her voice filled with exasperation.

I frowned, trying to remember something my mother had once said long ago. Something that I hadn't heard of since, but then it clicked.

"Gamma," I whispered.

She blinked up at me, her eyes wide. "A Gamma? Are you just saying Greek letters now for a Pack? Alpha, Beta, Heir, Healer, Enforcer, and Omega. Those are the only ones."

I shook my head, everything settling into place as if the moon goddess herself was whispering in my ear. "There's Foreseer. There's Tracker. There are maternals and elders. There are more than just those in the main hierarchy. But a *Gamma*. I've heard of one before. But I've never met one."

"And what is a Gamma wolf?" she asked, her eyes wet.

"Not a dominant, not a submissive. You don't lower your eyes to anyone, and you don't feel the need to do so unless you remember that you're supposed to, right?"

She took a step back, her face paling.

"It means *I'm broken*. It means my wolf doesn't

understand what it's supposed to do. That's why I'm here all the time, Chase. Don't you understand that? Why I fit in so much with the Aspens. Because I'm not supposed to slide into the Aspens. Because I'm not one of you. But I'm supposed to fit in with the Redwoods, and I don't. My wolf doesn't do what it's supposed to. I'm a Redwood Pack princess, and I don't do what I'm supposed to." Her voice drifted off, the panic in her spirit echoed in the eyes of her wolf.

She was breaking my heart, and my wolf pushed at me, wanting more. "Baby...you are wonderful and strong and can fit in anywhere you slide into. I *feel* it...and I think you're a Gamma."

Skye gave me an exasperated look. "And what is that exactly?"

"Not Greek, but lamb and wolf," I whispered. "The Gamma is one who is outside the hierarchy, the one who is there to put the broken pieces together."

Her eyes widened, and she shook her head. "Don't make things up to try to make me feel better about feeling like I don't belong. Don't."

"I'm not. I would never do that, Skye. Not to you, not to anyone else. A Gamma is a perfect balance for a broken Alpha." I hadn't meant to say those words, and when she paled again, I cursed under my breath.

"Maybe you're to find a Pack with a broken Alpha.

Someone like Cole, someone who needs help rebuilding their Pack."

My wolf snarled at me, annoyed I would bring up another Alpha even as I was standing right there. We had just made love in that fucking bed right behind me, and here I was, trying to push her to someone because I knew she couldn't be mine. How could she be my Gamma wolf, the balm to the broken ties that made me an Alpha, if she wasn't my mate? And I knew for a *fact* she couldn't be my mate.

So, what was I supposed to do with that? How was I supposed to put those pieces together?

Her eyes widened, and she stared at me, the hurt within the depths of her eyes reaching out to me. "*Cole.* You think that I'm this made-up term, a Gamma, because you can't think of anything else. You're trying to push me towards Cole, your friend, a wolf I have no connection to, because it makes things easier for you."

"A Gamma wolf is there to balance the Alpha. They're the Alpha's mate. That's what the stories used to be. Ask your parents. I'm sure they remember. The elders would too. You just don't see it that often because an Alpha's supposed to be strong."

"And you're calling Cole weak so you don't have to think about what's happening between us?" she asked softly.

"I'm not calling Cole weak. But the Centrals need

help. They're rebuilding from the ground up. What better than a Gamma wolf?"

"I am not Cole's mate!" she shouted.

"How would you know? You don't spend any time with him. Fuck, you could be Allister's mate, or Riaz's. Or any other Alpha out there." My wolf scrambled as I kept reaching for anything to make sense.

"But not you," she said, her voice breaking.

"You can't be."

She took a staggering step back, shaking her head. "You know what's happening with the shifters, Chase. You know that we're not finding mates the way that we used to. We're changing. Mating bonds can be hidden. Why can't we take that chance? Does this not feel real between us? You know it's different. Why isn't this different for you?"

"You're not my mate, Skye. I'm sorry. But I thought we knew this. You're not mine."

Every time I said the words, I felt like someone was killing me slowly. They were taking part of my future away, but I knew that was the truth. She wasn't mine. She could not be. That was the one thing I knew as fact, even as I knew that she had to be a Gamma, a wolf normally unheard of, but a balm to a broken Pack.

But it wasn't the Aspens. It couldn't be.

"Why do you know?" She paled even further. "You found your mate, didn't you? Oh, goddess, you've been with me, and you know who your mate is. That's why you're so sure—even with the magics of our world evolving. You know who your mate is. It's Malissa, isn't it? That connection. Oh, goddess. What have I done?" The blood leached from her face, and she turned, and I cursed under my breath.

"I don't know who my mate is. But I know it's not you."

And with those words, her wolf howled, mourned, and I knew I had broken what we'd had irrevocably.

I had broken this Gamma wolf.

Forever.

CHAPTER
FIFTEEN

Skye

I SCRAMBLED OUT OF THE HOUSE, NEEDING TO breathe. I'd known this. Of course, I had known this. Why was I acting like this? Acting as if I could change something.

"Skye. Come back." I moved away from Chase, needing just a moment.

Because I had done the unthinkable.

I had fallen in love with the Alpha.

I had done the one thing I promised myself I wouldn't do, bare myself, be open, and fall in love.

And I knew that was going to break me. Because

Chase wasn't mine, and he was so adamant that I wasn't his.

I should have been better. Stronger. And I wasn't. And that was on me.

"Skye."

"I need a minute," I called out, my hands shaking.

What was wrong with me? It wasn't like this was a surprise. We had both gone in knowing that we weren't for each other. From the start of our flirtations and seductions, he had known that I wasn't his.

Why was I acting as if I were surprised?

My goddess, I had made this problem. I had fallen for him. But he knew he couldn't do the same for me. I needed to believe that this was just sex, friendship, and comfort. And nothing else.

I hated myself, right then. *I hated myself.*

"Skye." He gripped my elbow, stopping me, and I whirled on him.

My wolf pushed at me, whimpering, angry, hurt. Everything all at once, and I couldn't keep up. This wasn't her fault. She was confused. Hurt. It was the human part of me that had hurt us both. That was somehow hurting Chase, too. "I'm sorry. I know that you're not mine. I know that. I'm sorry."

His eyes went gold as he studied my face, the desperation in them killing me. "Skye. I don't want to hurt you."

Hurt and anger slashed out of me, and I wasn't sure which would win. "You don't know who your mate is, but you *know* it's not me. So, something must tell you that, and *fine*. We're not mates. We're not each other's forever. I'll get over it, Chase." A lie. A damned lie. "Of course, I will. And you don't need to make up a position for me in the Pack so I can feel better about myself. I'm a big girl. I'll get over my feelings."

And once again, I felt like I was lying to myself, but I let that be. My wolf couldn't breathe.

Chase growled low. "I'm not fucking making up a Gamma. Ask the elders. Ask your parents. A Gamma is a perfect balance for a broken Alpha. I used to think they were a myth, but the way you can look into my gaze? The way you can push back against any wolf and seemingly can fit in anywhere that needs you, that's a Gamma."

Confusion warred with agony, and I couldn't fight them both. "Stop lying. I'm broken, I know that. It's okay. I've been this way my entire life, and I'm going to be this way until the end of my days. I'm a strong wolf. I might not be the best wolf out there, but I can fight. And that's all I'm good at. I'm fine with that."

"You know that's not the case."

"You aren't understanding me. I'm not a Gamma. Because a Gamma is, what, a perfect balance for a broken Alpha? A perfect mate for that broken Alpha. I don't want to be Cole's. I don't want to be Riaz's or Allister's. I don't want to be anyone else's but *yours*." And there. I said it. Why was I tormenting myself like this? "I don't want to be anyone's but *yours*," I repeated, my voice a broken whisper. "But I'm not yours, because you're so sure about that. You're even more sure than my wolf, and my wolf is confused. Just like always. So just let me be. Don't make up titles for me, don't push me off on anyone else. I can do that myself."

My breaths came out in ragged gasps as I struggled for control.

"I know that you're not mine because a Foreseer told me."

His blurted words caught me off-guard, and I stared at him, shaken to my core. "What?"

"When I was younger, a Foreseer told me I would die and become Alpha. That my mate would fade for me, and I would lose what I have. My mate would be of bone and blood. And I would see my mate and know her in truth. That is what she told me when I was fifteen years old."

"Chase," I croaked, my voice barely above a whisper. He said the words in a staccato as if he were just repeating them by rote, as if he didn't know what they truly meant—or didn't want to.

I wasn't sure what I wanted them to mean either.

"She told me that I would die, and I did. Not for long, but I did. I had to die for my father to be satisfied."

"Chase."

His eyes were wild, and the only thing I wanted to do was hold him close and lie to him, tell him everything would be okay. "No, let's get this out there. You should know. Because I feel something for you, Skye, but you *can't* be my mate. Don't you see that? I know who I'm supposed to be because a Foreseer told me, and everything so far has happened. I died because my father killed me, and then he forced me to come back. Over and over again. And later that day, he died. The Talons took him out, saved our world, and my dad died. And I became the Alpha of the Aspen Pack. All of that happened, just like she said."

"You died?" I stood there, the world quaking beneath my feet as I tried to come to terms with what he just told me.

"Yeah. My dad held me in a cage for over a decade. He sometimes let me out to trot me out as the Heir, but nobody knew who I was. I couldn't help my people, Skye."

My hands were on his chest, soothing his wolf, before I thought better of it. He didn't push me back. Instead, he lowered his head, pressing his forehead to mine.

"It's not your fault, Chase."

"I wasn't strong enough to protect our Pack. You think you're not strong enough? I think you're the strongest person I know. And I think you're a Gamma, even if you don't."

"This isn't about me. This isn't about a word that I still think you made up," I teased, though there was nothing jovial in my tone.

"I died because my father wanted to test his projects on me. Because he hated the way I looked."

"I'm sorry." My wolf howled, and tears slid down my cheeks.

"There's nothing for you to be sorry about. He hated his mate, my mother. It was a mating gone wrong, and somehow I ended up born into that messed-up life. I don't know who my father was before that. He could've been a good man, a good Alpha. Nobody will fucking talk about him, so I don't know. He broke their trust and corrupted who we were. He doesn't deserve a good memory. He doesn't deserve any kind words about who he was before he changed. If he even changed at all. He tortured me for over a decade, tortured and killed my friends. I'm the only one left of my family, of my line, and it was all written down in prophecy by a Foreseer that my father killed, too."

I knew the story of Blade and the Aspens, but not Chase. He'd held that to himself for far too long, and my heart broke with each word.

"Tell me the rest. Tell me, Chase."

He swallowed hard and looked at me, his eyes glowing gold with his wolf.

"My dad would put me in the cage for days at a time, only let me out to torture me before putting me back in. He cut me, whipped me, poured acid over my wounds to see if they would scar." He pulled off his shirt so I could see the lines on his chest, his back. The same lines I brushed my fingers over now, the same lines I had gently kissed the night before.

"It takes a lot for a wolf to scar. You know the former Omega of the Redwoods? The painful magic they used and the salt they used to keep those scars on his face and body? Same things. But he never touched my face." Chase let out a breath. "He wanted me to look like my mother, to see my mother's eyes when he hurt me. Because he hated her so much, and I never knew why. *I'll never know why.* My dad wanted power over me just like he wanted power over secrets in the Pack itself. He was trying to be the Alpha of the world, becoming a Supreme Alpha, even before I knew that those existed outside of myths. And so, he hurt me, and when I didn't scream anymore, when there was nothing left of me to hurt, he brought in Audrey and forced her to shift into her cat form and back." He let out a shaky breath. "He did things, more things I can't talk about. But he hurt Steele, Dara, and Wren. Hayes. All of them.

Everyone who was part of this Pack who hadn't been on my father's side. He hurt them in front of me, and there was nothing I could do. The look of shock on their faces when they realized I was alive and still there. The look of relief because I hadn't died, but it wasn't like I could come and help them. They had to have known something was wrong because there wasn't a new Heir, but he'd said I was dead, and the magic had forsaken the Pack. That was why there was no replacement Heir. He'd used dark magic to hide the bonds of Heir from the rest of the Pack. But, deep inside, I knew the truth. I was dead. Dead to them, dead with them. And there was nothing I could do."

My mouth went dry and I tried to think of what to say, what to do with all of this. I knew he'd been through hell, had seen the end of the abyss, and had survived. Yet, I hadn't realized how dark Blade had gone with his own son. If I could, I'd raise the damn Alpha again only to show him who his son had become before killing the asshole again.

Only, I couldn't do anything except prove to Chase he was stronger than his past.

And to do that, we had to look at the future.

"What about the prophecy? Say it again."

Chase studied my face, his wolf in his gaze, before he let out a breath. "He said my mate would fade for me. And I would lose what I had. What kind of fucking prophecy is that? That they'll *fade* for me? The person that I'm supposed to love and be with and connect with on a soul-deep basis with a bond that is unbreakable. They're supposed to fade for me and change? Fuck that. I don't want that for my mate. And I would lose what I have? What do I have now? I am building so much with this Pack. *We* are. I don't want to lose that again. I don't want to lose anything."

Tears threatened again, and I patted his chest, trying to think through the scramble of my thoughts. "I know. It's okay."

"It's not okay. My mate will be of bone and blood. Meaning born out of it? Born from the horror of war? Or will become that from being mated to me?"

I shook my head, just as confused as he was. "Chase. You know prophecies, sometimes they're just a bunch of words together that sometimes make sense in retrospect, and they're supposed to confuse you. Because if they tell you the truth as they see it, the whole truth with no changing, you become a self-fulfilling prophecy."

"Skye."

"And the last part?" I asked, swallowing hard as I ignored the sound of my name on his lips.

"You know the last, Skye. Why it hurts for me to even say this. Why I don't want to hurt you."

"That you will see your mate, and you will know her

in truth. That is why you know that I'm not yours. *Because you see me, but you know I'm not yours.*"

My wolf howled, and I saw the echo of Chase's in his gaze.

"Exactly. I'm sorry, Skye. So fucking sorry. But everything else has come true. I died, and I came back. And there's nothing I can change." He cupped my face, pressing his forehead to mine again. "I wanted it to be you, Skye."

And with that, my heart shattered into a thousand pieces, my breaths coming in choppy pants as I tried to hold on.

"I wish it was, too. I wish you were mine."

"I don't understand fate or the goddess or anything. Because I could see you at my side, us protecting our Packs together. I'm falling for you, Skye. But I can't let myself fall completely because I'll hurt you. Just like I hurt everybody else. And I can't do that."

"Well, this is touching," a voice said from the darkness and I whirled, my wolf alert, my claws sliding through my fingertips.

Chase let out a growl and snarled. "What the fuck are you doing here, Malissa? What do you mean?"

I started, confused at his use of the name *Malissa.* Because that acidic voice did not sound like the sweet woman I had gotten to know. The sweet woman that I was so afraid was Chase's true mate. The woman I was jealous of. And yet, as she came out of the darkness, her hair flowing around her chest, her leather corset tight, her leather pants clinging to her hips, I knew that this was the Malissa I had seen, I had known.

But something was wrong.

Malissa raised her chin. "You should have seen *me*. I just don't understand why you never *saw* me. I was the one with power. The one connected to our master." She snapped the words, and my wolf went on alert, my hands shaking.

I blinked, her words penetrating the fog of my pain. "It was you. You're the one who is making sure that the vampires always know where Chase is."

Everything clicked into place then. The fact that someone had told the vampires and hybrids where Chase would be on that first run when I saved him. And how they always seemed to know exactly where the Alpha was.

"Of course it was me. But they were never supposed to kill him. They were supposed to weaken him so I could be the one to take him to my master." She smiled and my wolf shook, anger nearly consuming me at the thought of what this woman had done.

My wolf paced, and I tried to figure out what the hell this woman was saying.

Chase snarled. "Why, Malissa? Why would you hurt your Pack?"

"A Foreseer told me that I would be bound with an Alpha. And yet, you never saw me. You should have. I tried to be sweet, tried to be the adorable little submissive that you wanted, instead, you went to *her*. A nothing with no title and no name. Then I realized who my true mate was. Never you. But my master." She flung her fingers at me, and magic burned into my skin.

She was wolf, but there was magic that tasted wrong, almost vampiric. I froze, fearful.

"Are you a hybrid?" I asked, the words tumbling from my lips as agony cascaded over my skin.

Malissa threw her head back and laughed. "No, I'm not one of those slobbering fools. I mean, they've been practicing so hybrids could get better. You'll just have to see. I mean, you will see soon. I'm not a hybrid, but Blade made sure that some of the witches were hidden. So I'm both—wolf, with just enough magic that the vampire sorcery doesn't work on me the way it will with you.

"You should have seen me, Chase. Because if you would've let the wolves take you that first time, you would be safe in my arms. At least...until I was through with you. Now my master will prove the true power."

"Malissa, what have you done?" Chase asked, moving forward.

"What I had to do. For the good of our people. You were never a good enough Alpha. I could've had you for an evening with my master, but you were never the Alpha I wanted, craved, or desired. Your father was that man. You were a second chance—a second *choice*. I don't choose you now. I choose the enlightenment coming from the great beyond. From those who promised me. From my master."

"Malissa," I called out, reaching forward.

There was something wrong with her, as if the magic had twisted her, and she wasn't speaking for herself anymore. I didn't know if this was her true feelings or something the vampires had done to her. But she had betrayed us all. Had nearly killed us, had hurt us, and now she wanted Chase.

I moved, trying to get to her, but Malissa just smiled, a smile that sent shockwaves of cold through my soul, and then she flicked out her hands.

Wind and power pummeled into me, knocking me off my feet. I screamed, smashing through the forest, being shoved through the air by this force I couldn't see or touch or taste or smell. I knocked into the trees, branches smashing into my back, cutting into me, and then I was pushed through the wards.

The magic cut into my skin, breaking and bleeding. I slammed into the ground, next to Chase, as we both tried to stand up, but then more magic pushed at us, blows hitting us one after another. I reached out to Chase, trying to catch my breath, trying to scream. An intense pressure squeezed at my throat, at my limbs, twisting as if I were in a vise.

Malissa smiled through the wards and waved her fingers. "The magic of the vampires was supposed to make you mine. To give me the power to lure you, and yet nothing. It didn't work because of *her*."

She threw her hands out, and blood seeped from her eyes, mouth, and nose.

The wards shone.

Magic with those black shards dug into my skin, Chase's too, as we crawled, trying to get to the wards and warn our people. But, like a soap bubble around the den, they pulsated red, and then nothing. They were still intact, but had she done something to weaken them? To scar them forever?

I didn't know because Malissa fell, a bright smile on her face as she lay in death.

I could hear others call out.

And then the magic pulsated again, shards of black digging into my skull.

And then there was darkness.

CHAPTER
SIXTEEN

Chase

HELL WAS BUT A MEMORY. LIFE SEEMED TO BE EVEN darker.

The cold metal and steel of the cage pressed against my back, and I had to shake myself awake, reminding myself that this wasn't a dream. This wasn't the past. No, this was indeed the future.

The present.

I couldn't see Skye. I couldn't see anything but the darkness and the bars surrounding me.

My wolf howled, pacing deep inside me, wanting out.

It's okay, old friend. We'll find a way out of this. We'll get to Skye. We did this before. We'll do it again.

My wolf had been the only one I could rely on for so many years. I hadn't been able rely on anyone else because if I had, I would end up hurting them in the end. So I hadn't let myself. I stayed away. Just like I was doing now. I would be stronger, because I had to be.

I took a deep breath, trying to remind myself that I could get through this. My wolf pushed, and I took in my surroundings. I was in a dark room, still stuck in a cage, but it was different than before. It was tall enough that I could stand, though I was still leaning against the wall, my legs weak from whatever had knocked me out. Hopefully, I would be able to get full function back soon, because I needed to find Skye.

"I see you're awake," a voice said from the darkness, and I stiffened, opening up my senses to figure out exactly who that was and what was going on.

The room smelled of mold and decay. It smelled wet, like we were underground.

I had never been to this place before. It didn't feel familiar. Nor could I feel the magic of the den anywhere close, meaning we had to be far away. I hoped the Pack would find us, but would stay safe in the process.

"Don't bother trying to reach out to your den and feel for your Pack. You won't be able to reach them. This has been a long time coming, Alpha. I suppose it's time to get to know each other."

The lights blinked on in that moment, nearly blinding me. I put my hand over my eyes to let them adjust, and then I stood up straight because I needed to be ready for anything.

Valac stood in front of me, his dark hair pulled back in a slick ponytail.

He wore black slacks, a black belt, and a stone-gray shirt that buttoned up to the collar. I found it odd that he was so buttoned up since he normally wasn't. Perhaps this was his torture look. Something that made him feel as if he were the one in power. And considering he most likely had the key to the cage I was locked in, he was the one with the power.

"What do you want, Valac?" I asked, my voice rough. It sounded as if it had been in disuse for a long time, which made me realize that I didn't even know what time it was. How much time had passed since Malissa betrayed us? *And had died in the process.* I could barely hold back my rage at the thought, because my wolf had known. There had always been something, a lure that she had put out to me, most likely from vampire magic. But it also wanted to know why. Why was she like that? Why had I been intrigued? It hadn't been natural. No, my wolf had always known she was a traitor, and yet we hadn't been able to voice that.

I let out a growl, just low enough to make Valac's eyes narrow.

"I see you're beginning to understand the ramifications of your situation. Well, let's get into it. You are here at my request. My master wants it too, and I would like to know more about you. Let's get to know each other, shall we?"

"Fuck you," I snapped.

"No, I don't think we will be doing that. But you are here because the Aspens will be mine. We need to cleanse the world of the so-called powerful shifters. Because you are not as strong and righteous as you think you are. Once we get rid of you, we are one step closer to ruling this dimension."

"You think killing me is one step closer to taking over the world? I've heard a few diabolical villain diatribes in my day, but you've lost your damn mind."

Valac sneered. "Perhaps I have, or perhaps Malphas is the one who brought me to true salvation. And taught me the power of the blood in our veins. You were blessed by an amorphous glob that doesn't even come down to grace you with her presence. You call that a blessing? I call it a curse. My master stands with us. Where is your so-called goddess? Not here. No. She is nowhere to be seen when you are going to be bleeding and begging for salvation."

"So now you're going to be in a fight with the

goddess. I see you've truly lost your mind." I wasn't trying to antagonize him, but the more that I angered him, the more he spoke. The more he would tell us of their plans. Maybe if we could figure out how the fuck they were using this magic of theirs and where they had gotten it from, we could find a way to fight against it.

And I needed to find Skye.

"You think you're cute. You think you're the one in power, but you haven't been for a long time. You don't even have the strength to fight our wards. You can't sense the betrayal within your den. You can't fight the shards of magic. And you won't be able to fight when I turn your precious little bitch into a hybrid."

I snarled then, taking a step forward without even meaning to. "Let her go. This is between you and me."

Valac just grinned widely. "No. It's not. We will use you as a symbol of our power and sacrifice, but you are not the one in control here. And this fight isn't between you and me. You are nothing. We know who the true power is, and it will never be you. And we will use the little wolf of the Redwoods to prove that."

"Let her go."

"The answer is simple. No." Valac moved to the side, and a large metal door squeaked open, the grating metal against metal slicing into my ears as it echoed through the room. Two sentient vampires moved forward, rolling a metal gurney between them. My wolf bucked at the reins and I leapt forward, nearly pressing myself against the metal bars. But I knew those metal bars were coated in that vampire magic. The dark shards that would cut into my skin. I could sense it along the metal, and I wasn't going to weaken myself for him. But I knew who they had on that gurney, and I wanted to growl, to scream.

Sunny, the vampire's mate, walked in, her stroll sensuous grace as she rolled her hips and slid her hands down the front of her leather jumpsuit.

"Now I do believe this is where we have fun, don't you think?"

Skye was unconscious on the gurney, wearing scrubs that weren't hers. She was bruised and bloody, with metal manacles around her neck, wrists, thighs, and ankles.

They're going to hurt her, and I couldn't get through these fucking bars.

"Now, that's the wolf we want to see in your gaze. Look at you, so worried about your dearest woman. But not your mate. Malissa was very confident in the fact that she's not yours. Interesting, because all you seem to do is fuck this bitch, and yet you don't get to keep her. She isn't blessed by the dear goddess you treasure so much."

"Let her go," I whispered, my voice low, dangerous.

"The answer is no," Sunny teased. "In fact, let's

wake her up. I do enjoy the taste of fear in the air. It makes the blood that much sweeter."

I gripped the bars, the magic slicing into my skin, red hot pokers of pain jamming into my hands, but I ignored it, trying to pull the bars apart. I was strong, my wolf stronger than most. I could get through this. They weren't bonded by witch magic, but by vampire magic. Maybe I could get through, like I hadn't been able to before with my father.

"Wake her up," Sunny directed, her voice still in that sing-song tone.

The vampire to Skye's left grinned, his eyes narrow red slits, as he slowly sliced his claw down Skye's arm.

"Don't you fucking touch her!" I roared.

"We just need her awake, dearest," Sunny whispered as she slid her arm around Valac's waist and leaned against his shoulder. "As soon as she's awake, we can tell you a little bit more. It's no fun to have an audience of one."

The vampire slid a knife out of his sheath and began to slowly, methodically cut runes into Skye's skin.

My wolf raged at the sight of her blood. I roared, trying to get through the damn bars that kept me caged.

"Now, we're close. So close. Don't you want to see how a hybrid is made?" Sunny asked.

I slammed against the bars, magic slicing into me, but I ignored the pain. I needed to get out. "Skye. Fight."

As soon as I said her name, her eyes slid open. She screamed, her body bowing from the table as much as the metal manacles allowed her.

The vampire kept cutting into her skin, one slice after another.

"Let. Her. Go." I bit out the words, my wolf at the edge. "Use me instead."

"Enough," Sunny said as she held up a hand. The vampire stepped away as blood slowly seeped from Skye's wounds.

She looked up at me, her eyes wide, and I pushed closer, ignoring my skin's singe, the smell of burnt skin and hair.

"Fight, Skye. I'll get you out."

Her eyes were wild, her wolf at the forefront, and I was so afraid that we would lose her, maybe not as a hybrid, but by going rogue. There was no Skye in there, just fear and pain and her wolf.

"Malissa said that you thought she was a Gamma," Valac said.

My wolf growled at the sound of the traitor's name. "Let her go. She has nothing to do with this."

"She has everything to do with this," Sunny put in. "A Gamma is the balance for a broken Alpha. And who better to be broken than you, Alpha Aspen."

"I'm going to fucking gut you," I growled.

Valac beamed. "That's what they all say, and yet I'm

the one with the bloody bodies at my feet, and I'm still standing here, not a mark on me."

That was a lie. The vampire had a scar on his face from Audrey and Gavin. This wasn't the end. I wasn't going to let it be the fucking end.

"A Gamma as a hybrid would be amazing, a boon. Because if you unbalance the balance, all that is left is chaos." Sunny beamed.

"Do you know why we are vampires?" Valac asked, and I stilled, letting my wolf be the one in control for a moment. He was stronger. All I wanted to do was scream and break my way out, even though my hands were burned, my body bleeding from trying to get to Skye. She had stopped shaking and just lay there, her eyes wide, as she slowly came to the forefront of her consciousness. She was trying to find a way out, even in pain, but I didn't know how to do this. Not until they gave us an opening. I met Skye's gaze and hoped to hell she would be able to hold on that much longer.

"Tell me about yourself then," I said calmly, so calm I knew that they could hear the steel beneath. I needed to let them talk so Skye and I would have a chance.

"When Caym walked through the portal after the sacrifice that brought him here, he unraveled everything for us. The demons from their realm came forward to pull Caym back once he was defeated. Because Caym was weak. He wasn't like our master. When Malphas came back to the human realm, he had a plan. Where Caym was weak, relying on wolves alone to create power, Malphas knew he needed his children. Us."

"The vampires," I whispered.

"The vampires," Sunny agreed.

Valac smiled. "Your moon goddess created wolves. The sun and midnight goddess created the bears and cats. But our god, our master, created us. We are his children, the ones that will roam the earth as masters ourselves. We will bring forth a new world in which a power of blood and bone are the sacrifice that must be made. We will be the ones who live in power and strength. And the shifters and those magic-born who do not bow to us will learn what it means to fight against us. Your people have been on this earth for centuries, and yet you have hidden for so long. You fight shifter against shifter, Pack against Pack. There is no harmony. And without that harmony, you can't build the power you need to. You can't fight who you need to."

He sounded like a madman, but there was knowledge to his words, a danger behind the power that worried me more than the insanity. "So, you want to rule the world and kill us. You've said this before, Valac. What's new?"

"What's new is that we're one step closer. Closer than you'll ever know. It took us less than three decades to build our army, to create magic that you could never beat. And soon, we will have more hybrids, shifters turned vampire, in our army. We will be unstoppable. And that is why we need you, Blade's son. Because you were always the traitor's son, and you will be the traitor now."

"I'll never do what you want," I snarled.

"You don't have the power to fight. To save this woman you were going to toss away because she's not yours. Well, she's mine now. As are you." Valac moved, the knife in his hand shining underneath the light. It was coated in that same magic, and when he slid it into my gut, his movement so quick I didn't even have time to move, I roared, my wolf at the front.

"The torture that your father bestowed upon you, the torture that Malissa went over in aching detail with me, was just the beginning. I will mark your skin with each blow that he gave you, and then I will turn you and your precious bitch to hybrids. I will send you back to the Aspens, and you will kill those in your charge, those who are too weak to fight. And those who are strong enough to take you down will be demoralized by having to kill their Alpha. By another betrayal. And then the Aspens will be no more, and finally, the wolves will know who their masters are."

Valac twisted the knife, and Skye screamed.

CHAPTER
SEVENTEEN

Skye

METAL MANACLES BIT INTO MY SKIN, AND I PUSHED, trying to get free, agony searing up my side from the wounds.

"It'll be better when he starts bleeding, where we can use that blood for the hybrid. He doesn't realize it yet, but he will be our future."

Sunny prowled around the cage, her eyes glowing red. But she was in full control. She might look like she wanted only blood, but I wasn't sure what else she wanted.

Chase fell to the ground, his knees hitting the

concrete floor with a sickening thud. He looked up at me, his eyes gold as blood seeped from his side, his mouth, his nose. They were hurting him, shoving magic into his body, and trying to torture him in front of me. They brought out the whip and another blade, as other vampires walked into the room, ready to torture the man that I loved.

"Stop it. This isn't going to get you anywhere."

They froze and stared at me while Chase looked at me as if he wanted me to stop. Wanted me to be quiet, so maybe I could find a way out of here. But that wasn't going to happen. Not without each other. Everything ached. The symbols that they carved into my skin hurt, and I wanted to get out of here. I tried to breathe and figure out if I could do anything but sit there and bleed. So I needed them distracted. I needed to find another way out of here, or perhaps give our Packs enough time to find us.

"Do you know how a vampire feeds?" Sunny asked as she walked towards me, trailing her fingers up my arm. I shivered, but it had nothing to do with pleasure or cold, but fear and revulsion.

"You're a bloodsucker. I'm pretty sure I can figure that out."

"You're so cute. The fangs aren't needed to suck blood through like little straws. No, we bite, tear using our fangs, and then keep our fangs in because of the pain and the pleasure. There's so much pleasure in someone's fang. You've never felt anything better than when you're breaking into someone's skin, sucking their blood down your throat and swallowing hard, your fangs pulsing."

I cringed, wondering why it looked as if Sunny was about to get off just talking about it.

"I don't think I need to hear about you getting a fang job. Just let us go. There's nothing we can do for you."

"If there was nothing you could do for us, you would be dead. But there's something. We need blood to survive. And I want your blood. Shifter blood. It's so much stronger than a human's. Oh, sometimes not as strong as a witch. I think it depends on the witch. Witch blood is so tasty."

Sunny licked her lips and I held back a shudder.

"And when they're screaming and needing release, just trying not to die in agony, I'm there to help them along. I've never turned a witch into a vampire before. I don't know exactly what would happen, but I want to find out. You're not a witch. Neither is the man bleeding out for you. But you *are* a shifter. And when I get you near death, after we finish carving the runes into your skin, your pain and blood along with my bite, over and over all over your body, will change you into a hybrid. And hybrids are *strong*, stronger than a shifter, but under *my* control."

So that was how they made hybrids. I remembered the one who had been sent to us to die, and I refused to become what that poor soul had been.

Sunny grinned. "I will do everything in my power to break you. To show the world that I will be its master, along with my master and with my mate. We are stronger than you will ever be. And now you'll understand the pain that we can cause. The pain that we can bring with a single bite."

She moved my hair from my neck, right above the manacle, winked, and then licked across my throat. I tried to move away, but I was pressed down into the metal table, unable to do anything other than lie there as she gently sucked on my neck.

"This is where the mate mark would be, correct? Or is it a little lower?" She licked across my shoulders, gently scraping her fangs but not breaking the skin. "Not that you *have* a mate mark. No, you'll never get one because you aren't mated. That little Alpha over there isn't your mate. He just wanted to fuck you, and when he was done with you, and you were all used up and worthless, he'd walk away. He'd find his mate. You were just something to fuck hard into the ground when he couldn't handle his own wolf." She clucked her tongue. "No mate mark for you. But I can give you another mark."

She moved like a viper, pinning me to the metal

table as she slid her fangs into my shoulder, biting down with a ferocity that made me scream. It ripped a roar from my throat, and I tried to move away, the tearing of my skin echoing in my ears as she sucked on my blood, biting down harder.

"Let go of her!" Chase shouted from the cage. I couldn't see him. I could only hear him as he thrashed against the metal bars. They were shaking, rattling against the wall as others shouted. They were whipping him, throwing things at him, magic and metal and anything they could to try to hurt him. The scent of burning flesh hit my nostrils, and I knew it was the magic burning his skin as he was trying to get to me. I tore against the table within my bonds, trying to get away. I was bruised and bleeding at each part I was held down, but Sunny continued to suck, to bite down and ravage my flesh. I knew if I got out of this, I would have a scar on my shoulder.

My vision began to dim, and I swallowed hard before Sunny moved away and licked my wounds closed. At least as much as she could because she had torn my flesh wide. I could feel the blood seeping down my chest, into my shirt. Sunny looked down at me and licked her lips.

"So strong and fresh. Full of power. Is this what a Gamma is? Will I gain your powers? I just don't know. I need to try it out. To see exactly what happens when I sip from different sources. I want to know their powers."

Valac cleared his throat. "Now, Sunny, don't give them all of our secrets."

"So, you want our powers? That's why you want us. It's not just our strength." My voice was hoarse, my screams having ravaged my throat just as much as Sunny's fangs had my shoulder.

Sunny tossed her hair and laughed. "Maybe. You'll never know. You'll be dead or under my control long before that. If you survive the shift."

"This is only the beginning, my mate," Valac whispered, before he kissed Sunny hard on the mouth, my blood being shared between them. Revulsion echoed through me, and I tried to pull away from the bonds, causing the metal to dig deeper into my skin, and there was nothing I could do.

I wasn't strong enough for this, and it didn't matter that I was Gamma. Chase had loosened the cage walls, that much I knew, but I didn't want him to kill himself for me.

I met his gaze, golden and fierce.

"I'll get you out," he mouthed.

I looked at him then, tears springing from my eyes as I tried to get free, blood pouring from my open wound.

"I love you," I mouthed, afraid that was the only time I would ever be able to say it.

His eyes narrowed, and he bucked at the walls again, trying to get free.

But then Sunny was in front of me, grinning.

"More runes, Brian. More runes, more blood, and then she will be mine."

Brian, the vampire at my side, dug into my skin and I screamed, trying to get away, but they held me down. It took four of them, but they were carving more symbols into my skin as Sunny chanted magic. She bit down on my arm, then my leg, then my neck, she just kept biting, and Chase was yelling, and I couldn't get out. There was nothing I could do.

And then Sunny's eyes went red and she grinned.

"One more bite, and you're mine. A hybrid."

And then I opened my mouth and howled as my life began to drain from me, but it wasn't only my howl filling my ears.

I joined Chase in the wolf's call, and I hoped to the goddess that this wasn't the end.

CHAPTER
EIGHTEEN

Chase

I PULLED AT THE BARS, RAGE FLOWING THROUGH ME as I howled, the sound twining with Skye's. They were hurting her. Biting her, and I knew she was one or so bite away from death or turning into a fucking hybrid. I would not let that happen. She thrashed against her bonds, and my wolf screamed, and I followed.

And just like that, my heart beat once, twice, and I *knew*.

Words from the past slammed into me, and the veil of secrecy and death fell away.

The prophecy had been right.

I had been wrong. Because I looked at the woman and my wolf *knew*.

I would lose her, and she was mine.

My mate.

The mating urge slammed into me abruptly, slicing at my skin, my heart.

She was mine. My mate, and she was dying because I could not get out and save her.

I gripped the bars, the magic within them burning my skin, the acrid scent of burned flesh in my nostrils. I let out a growl, the mating urge pulsating between us, and I knew. I knew if I did not get out of here soon, at this very instant, I would lose her. I would lose the woman I loved.

I wasn't going to let that happen. I pulled with every inch of my being, pulling at the bonds that made me Alpha.

I couldn't do this often and not without strain and power, but I *pulled*.

From Cruz and his bright darkness of Heir.

From Steele and his determined power as Enforcer.

From Audrey and her selfless sacrifice as Beta.

From Gavin and his bountiful strength as Tracker.

From Hayes and his vengeful pain as Omega.

From Wren and her quiet agony as Healer.

They, in turn, pushed what they had at me without

hesitancy, a trust in their Alpha that took me out at the knees.

The magic strained, the metal twisting, as others were shouting, trying to keep me back, but I ignored them. I ignored all of them for now.

I put all of my horror, pain, and strength, memories of the last time I was in a cage, and the helplessness I felt from being in this position again. It didn't matter that this wasn't the exact place I had been caged. That place had been burned to the ground.

No, none of it mattered. The memories were a stark fear, a lie that twisted inside my brain as I tried to get out.

I pushed, pulled, and as the wolf came forward, my claws sliding out of my fingertips, my voice strained as I pushed.

And finally, the first bend in the metal echoed in my ears, and then the next, and the next.

Others were screaming for me, trying to get near me, but the wolf saw nothing.

My mate was hurt, and I would be damned if anybody touched her again.

I tugged on the metal with all my will, muscles bulging, a shout echoing in the chamber. There were vampires all around, but all I could see was Skye on the table, screaming, bleeding.

I would not let her turn.

I could sense her heart beating quickly and then slower, slower.

Turning a wolf into a hybrid was like changing a human into a wolf. They had to be near death, and her heart was slowing.

I didn't know what would happen if she fully turned, and I would not let that occur.

So I let my wolf free.

The metal screeched, and then there was an explosion of power and strength, and I turned, shredding through my clothes, muscles bulging, bones breaking, tendons snapping. I growled and landed on all four paws, my wolf at the forefront.

I wasn't going to turn rogue, but I was using all of my strength at once.

Somebody shouted and I ripped into them, my fangs sliding into their throat. I ripped it out, then pounced on the next one, going through all of them with a fierce determination.

I would not let Skye die.

Skye looked at me then, her eyes wide, and then she growled, a fierce growl that sent Sunny scrambling back. I pounced on the next vampire, ripping its throat out, and then moved towards Skye. The bond between us was only partially complete because we hadn't marked each other.

But there was a bond. She was my mate. We just

needed to finish it. And I would. I would mark her as mine, and she would do the same to me. But for now, because we had made love, because we claimed each other as humans, we were one step closer. I fed her all the strength that I could through the bond, even as I fought my way through the vampires. The magic shone between us, dancing along the partially made bond. Skye's eyes glowed gold, and then she threw her head back and roared, snapping up her arms and her legs. She broke through the metal barriers, her body full of rage, and I could sense it.

I knew she was in pain. I knew she was bleeding, nearly dying, but she had so much rage mixed with mine, and she crouched on the metal bed, snarling.

"What? How?" Sunny asked, and then Skye jumped, slashing her claws towards the female vampire.

I tried to get to her and help, but then Valac and two more vampires were in front of me. I pounced, slashing at the closest vampire and killing it in one blow. Whoever these vampires were, they weren't good fighters. They weren't the ones that had fought us before. No, these were the underlings, and Valac was the true prize.

"I'll kill her. You hurt me? I'll kill her."

I lifted my lips into a snarl, showing fang. Valac was in vampire form, his fangs out, his eyes red.

"I will gut her where she stands. You might think you're strong, but you are nothing."

I pounced, ripping into Valac's arm. Valac pushed at me, punching and raking his claws down my side. I bit down again, clawing, trying to get towards Skye.

Skye was in human form, blood seeping down her arms and sides from her bite marks. She swayed, but her claws were out as she slashed at Sunny repeatedly.

"You never get to touch me again. Never get to hurt me." She kept shouting the words, but all I knew was that I needed to get her out of here.

Skye fell to her knees as Sunny pounced, trying to claw at Skye.

But the mating bond surged between us, and I pushed Valac down and ripped at the man's shoulder. I stomped on his face, clawing him, and moved towards Skye, throwing my entire body down on top of Sunny. Sunny screamed, and I clawed at her before Skye fell to the ground, her eyes wide, her body convulsing.

If I didn't get her out of here, she would turn into a hybrid, and there was no coming back from that.

"Chase," she whispered.

Blood seeped from her mouth. I slashed my claws down Sunny's side and she screamed. People were moving all about, but I nudged at Skye, trying to lift her up.

It would've been easier for me in human form, but

I'd shifted when I'd had so much rage within me that hadn't had anywhere to go. So I pulled on the bonds that made me Alpha and shifted to human in an instant of torture, somehow knowing I could.

I had never moved that fast, and the pain was excruciating. And from the look on Skye's face, she hadn't expected me to move with that speed either.

"Chase," she whispered.

"I've got you."

I picked up a metal pipe nearest to me and slammed it out, breaking the cheekbone of the nearest vampire. I picked up Skye, holding her close as she tried to walk beside me, but she was too weak. I used the metal and hit again and again, and then I ran towards the window and threw us through it.

We were only on the first floor, and the glass didn't break completely. Shards bit into my skin, but I covered Skye, and she was safe.

"Chase, the mating bond. You shifted." She kept coughing up blood, and I cursed before I picked her up and cradled her to my chest.

My wolf was at the forefront, guiding us toward the scent of Pack. Again, the moon goddess and the Pack bonds were guiding us. It was the only thing I had.

"Chase, I can walk. I'm healing."

I looked down at her again and frowned. I was naked, having torn through my clothes when I shifted.

She was wearing nothing more than scraps, covered in blood, but the wounds were indeed healing.

"Are you okay?" I cupped her face and lowered my forehead to hers. "Fuck, of course, you're not okay. We have to run. We have to get towards the Pack."

"I know. How did we, how did we break through all of that?"

I shook my head, trying to get my thoughts in order. Only a few things made sense to me in that moment, so I shared what I knew. "You settle me. You're Gamma. You fight because you're stronger. And we fought against the dark magic and vampire wards because we're together. Because we fight together. They're going to be angry and come after us, but we'll get to the den. But I found you."

"Chase," she whispered.

"I found you. I will always find you." I kissed her, my breath coming in shaky pants.

"I believe you." She let out a breath. "Let's go home. Everything hurts."

My wolf came out then, my voice a growl. "I'll kill them."

"And I'll help you. But we need to get healthy first. You're hurt." She ran her hands down my face. "I don't like you hurt."

"Same here, mate," I growled.

Her eyes widened, and I crushed my mouth to hers,

just for a moment. I needed to know she was there. It soothed my wolf enough that I wouldn't go rogue, but I still needed that anchor because we needed to move. So, I gripped her hand and we ran, faster than I'd ever run before, towards our den.

Perhaps another Alpha would have stayed, but I needed to protect my mate, and I needed to get to the den because our Pack needed us. And I needed them. If I stayed, I'd fail. It would be smarter to be with the Pack.

I made our way towards the edge of the barrier, where there was a group of trees, and I scented a familiar wolf that nearly made me grin.

"Fuck," I growled, and Skye nearly tripped.

"Is that...?"

She sounded weaker than she had before, so I turned to the side and picked her up again, cradling her to me.

"Knew they would be here."

And out of the trees, Gavin and Steele slid out, the darkness releasing them. They were covered in all black, the Tracker and my Enforcer.

"Well, it looks like we don't need to break you out," Gavin stated, his voice purposely light.

"Threats?" Steele asked, straight to business as usual.

"Not sure if they're coming. We need to get Skye to a Healer."

Gavin nodded tightly. "Wren wanted to come, but we nixed that idea." He looked over at Steele, who let out a snarl.

"You know she comes after it's finished, and we're the ones who finish it. I've got a first aid kit. And a set of clothes for you since I didn't think the bastards would let you keep yours."

"I just want to get home," Skye whispered, and Steele looked between us, his eyes widening. The first time he actually had a reaction that wasn't pure anger.

"Well fuck. It looks like the Aspens are going to be your home now."

Gavin smiled quickly before he looked over our shoulders. "Let's get you guys home before they follow. I scent vampires."

"I'm going to fucking kill them," I growled.

Both men nodded, and Skye echoed my growl. "We'll do it together. But first, let's get you healthy and whole. Come on, Alpha."

And then, because I was bleeding, my hands just now starting to hurt again from touching so much magic, I let Gavin hold Skye.

It was only because the other man was mated that my wolf was able to calm down. The other man seemed to understand that, and he nodded slightly, lowering his gaze, as he held a nearly unconscious Skye.

I could feel her across our partially woven bond. She

wasn't healthy yet. Wasn't whole. But she would be. I would make sure of it.

And then we would finish our bond and take care of those who threatened us.

They had threatened my mate, my Pack, and I'd be damned if I let them do it again.

CHAPTER
NINETEEN

Skye

By the time we made it to Chase's home, I was exhausted and shaking. My body was healing itself, albeit slowly. I could feel the magic of the Alpha bonds flowing through me, the partial bond between Chase and me pulsing.

We weren't fully bonded yet. It would take the mating mark to complete the bonding, but we were almost there.

Somehow, through our own pain and need for each other, we had unveiled the fact that we were mates to each other. We had pulled that shroud from our eyes, and we were whole. It still shocked me, and I wasn't quite used to the thought, and I didn't know if I ever would be.

As Chase was so dominant and an Alpha, his side of the bond was heady, full of strength. I could sense the tendrils that connected him to his Pack as Alpha. Yet I still felt my connection to the Redwoods. Those bonds weren't gone yet, because I wasn't fully Aspen.

I was in a space of two connections, a limbo, and I didn't know if anyone had ever felt like this before. I didn't know if anyone was supposed to feel like this but, considering how our mate bond had shown up out of nowhere, perhaps everything had been changing with the magic of mating bonds all along.

Even Chase had shifted quickly, without going through the pain and agony of a true long shift.

Instead, he had done something that I'd only heard of in the past and seen with one of my cousins. Chase had made an instant shift and protected me long enough for me to gain the strength to protect him back.

"Your Healers are on their way, as is Wren," Gavin said as he knelt in front of me, a smile on his face. I knew he was trying to soothe my worry, and I was grateful for it, but everything hurt, and I just wanted to make sure Chase was safe.

"Were the vampires following us?" Chase asked as he limped towards me. We had gone to Chase's place rather than the Healer's, and I had the feeling it had more to do with Chase needing to be at home, surrounded by his territory, rather than anywhere else. If we had been thinking clearly, I was sure he would've forced me to go directly to the Healer.

As soon as I thought that, Mark and Hannah, our Redwood Pack Healers, burst through the door, along with Wren. Wren was so much smaller than the others, even though my Aunt Hannah was tiny as well. Wren just looked delicate, as if she couldn't hurt a fly, but she was a lynx and a brilliant Healer.

Steele snarled. "The vampires followed us at first, and then they retreated, as if they were called back to whatever hell they need to go."

"Like *actual* hell?" Gavin asked.

Steele shook his head. "I meant metaphorical. I wished they would go back to their hell."

"So, I see you had an adventure," Hannah said as she smiled softly at me. Like the original hierarchy, Hannah didn't have her total connections to the Pack through her Healing bonds anymore. She still could heal because that's who she was, however, she was an earth witch who cared for her Pack and family. But it was Mark who was the one blessed by the goddess now, the one with the responsibilities. It was an odd dichotomy, and I still didn't understand how they worked together, just like how my cousins, uncles, and aunts worked as a unit. But it made us stronger.

Or, perhaps it made the Redwoods stronger, because I would be Aspen now.

I was Chase's mate.

I looked over Hannah's shoulder at Chase, who gave me a small smile as if he was just as shocked as me.

"The vampires tried to turn her into a hybrid. We stopped them, but I think it's only because Skye's a Gamma that she could burn through the compulsions and the bites."

Hannah's eyes widened, and then Wren cursed under her breath. "I can feel you, Skye, with my bonds with the Aspens, but faded. What about you, Mark?"

My cousin looked at me then, put his hand on my arm, and closed his eyes. Warmth spread through me, soft, sweet. My cousin was a gentle soul, born to be a Healer. "You're right. I can sense she's of two Packs for now." He gave me a small smile as he opened his eyes. "This might be the last time I can heal you like this without using my medical degree."

"Your parents are going to be happy, other than the fact that you almost died and were nearly turned into a hybrid," Hannah snapped, then shook her head. "Sorry. Why don't they work on you, and I'll go see if there are any cuts and scrapes I can work on for this Alpha over here before Wren gets there."

"So, what happened exactly when we were gone?" Chase asked as Hannah did just that. He smiled down at my aunt as she cleaned up the blood on his arms and hands so she could get the lay of the land.

"First, Gamma?" Gavin asked, his eyes wide. "As in, the mythological wolf that can calm an Alpha? I thought those were Omegas but special with crowns or something," he muttered.

That made me burst out laughing before I winced, the pain in my rib spreading.

Wren shook her head and then held hands with Mark as the two of them somehow blended their healings together to help me.

"I've never seen it work that way," Hannah said after a moment. "Wren and Mark working together on a wolf of two Packs. I know it won't always be like this because the mating isn't complete, but one day, perhaps when all four of our Packs are blended so seamlessly, we'll be able to heal with the magics that we have for more than just each other. And as for Gammas, I thought they were a myth, too. I remember reading about them back in your grandfather's study," Hannah said as she looked at me.

My heart raced as tears pricked my eyes. The thought of our four Packs working as a unit, of my grandfather's study that was now my uncle's, and then, of course, this new power that I supposedly held. "Am I really a Gamma? I'm not broken?" I whispered the words, afraid to even say them aloud.

Everyone started grumbling at the same time as Chase cursed under his breath and limped toward me. Wren let out a curse herself and then went over to Chase and began Healing him as Mark and Hannah finished on me.

"You are not broken," Chase snarled.

"I'm figuring that out now. I'm sorry, your Alphaness."

Steele chuckled, the sound rough from his throat. "I like that. We're going to have to use that."

"No, you won't. It's only for my mate," Chase said, possessive. "You're a Gamma, Skye. You balance me. You'll balance this Pack."

"It makes sense," Gavin said into the awkward silence. "What?" he asked as we all looked at him. "You could look all of us in our eyes, even though you're not as dominant as us. But you're also not submissive either. You're always where you need to be, protecting even though sometimes you throw yourself into any situation without looking. It's novel. I like it. A Gamma. And honestly, with the way that our Pack is trying to rebuild itself from the ashes, we need you. Hell, while I'm sad for the Redwoods to lose you, I'm glad that we're getting a new Packmate who can help us. Anything for Pack. And anything to fuck with those vampires." He winced as he said it, and I knew he was trying to dial down the tension in the room.

My cousin Mark looked up at me and smiled softly. "You'll always be Redwood at heart." He rolled his eyes at Chase's soft growl. "Sorry. Once born a Redwood, always a Redwood, even if you're bonded to the Aspens. An Alpha's mate. Look at you, being all nice and shiny. Just like Brie."

He smiled as he said it, speaking of our cousin, who was mated to the Talon Pack Alpha.

"I guess we just need to marry a Redwood into the Central Pack, and we've got the perfect connections," Hannah added as she looked around at the others in the room. "I know some of our Pack and yours are waiting outside to figure out what happened, and since you are as healed as we can get you for now, I'll let you discuss Pack security or whatever you need. But things are changing. We may not have the attacks happening on our soil as much as you are, but we're here to fight. And to protect." She cupped my face, kissed me softly on the cheek, then did the same to Chase, surprising him. "Welcome to the family, Chase." And then she walked out of the room, Mark following her, leaving three large, dominant, and growling men stunned in silence.

"That's my Aunt Hannah," I said with a laugh.

Wren just grinned. "She is mated to two men, the

first triad in a century. She knows how to bring down the house."

I laughed at Wren's words as the men shook themselves out of their stupor.

"Tell me what happened after we were taken," Chase ordered as he began to pace.

Somehow, even though I still ached slightly, the Healers had worked their magic. I had a feeling that we healed quickly not only because of the Healers, but the new mating had sent energy along the bond that was still only partially done. I didn't think it would ever happen like that again, or perhaps it would once we were fully mated. My wolf wanted to complete the mating, but there were things to do first. We needed to protect Pack first.

"We felt the world pulse that red and dark magic when you were taken," Steele began as Chase wrapped me in a blanket. I cursed at him, not wanting to look weak in front of the others, but honestly, I liked being taken care of, even when I knew this wasn't the end.

"What did it feel like?" I asked. "Everything's a bit hazy about that for me."

Steele shook his head. "It was as if the connections that we felt through the wards, the ones that protected us from the explosion, burned. Dara and Lily don't believe that the magic hurt the wards at all. We even had some of the Redwood witches over to make sure."

"What was it, then?" Chase asked, and I nodded, needing to know as well.

"We think it's the excess energy that she used to push you through it, whatever dark magic that she used. It might have been vampire magic. It might have been sacrificial dark magic. We might not ever know unless they use it again." Gavin shuddered.

"It felt like someone was ripping at my heart, pushing me through the damn thing. And then we passed out," Chase growled. "As if I wasn't a fucking Alpha."

"Honestly, I think if the two of you weren't as strong as you are, it wouldn't have worked the same. Skye, you *are* strong. You're a fucking Gamma apparently," Steele added. "But if you weren't as strong as you are, you would've died."

At that chilling remark, I reached out and gripped Chase's hand. He looked down at our clasped hands, and I knew his wolf was pricking in his skin for mine. But we needed to get through this. To breathe first. The mating urge rocked at me, and I knew that the others probably could tell, but we had to make sure the Pack was safe first.

Then we could finish the bond and get everything that I never knew that I could have, want, or desire.

"After you were taken, we went on alert, the soldiers and lieutenants near you were running towards your aid, but you were already gone. Those damn personal wards are too much." Steele shook his head.

"We're going to find a way through them. We will. We've already been able to fight through some of the compulsions and to get through the magics in that cage," I added, after explaining how we had gotten out of Sunny and Valac's clutches.

"Not soon enough for me," Steele added.

"Damn straight," Chase agreed.

"We found Malissa's body," Gavin spat. "At first, we thought she was injured right along with you, and then Dara scented the magic and screamed, since some of the magic was still in the air and tried to attach to her."

I stood up, my blanket falling at my feet. I ignored Chase's scowl since he wanted me to sit down again. "Is Dara okay?"

Steele nodded. "She is. Thankfully. But whatever the vampires used, their magic is attached somehow to death magic. I don't know exactly how, and neither does she, but we're trying to solve it. Apparently, it just takes time," he growled. He said the words as if he'd heard them often enough. Probably from Dara herself.

"We are stronger than the vampires know," I said softly as all three men looked at me. "I know we have to go over this repeatedly with the other members of the Pack, and my Pack, the Redwoods, and everyone else, and we will. But for now, we're okay."

Steele shifted on his feet. "My lieutenants just texted," he said, holding up his phone. "They checked out the place you were held. It's empty. They were long gone."

Chase cursed under his breath, and I sat up and wrapped my arms around his waist. My wolf soothed him as his shoulders relaxed, and I let out a breath.

My wolf nudged at the bond, wanting to help. "We knew they weren't going to stay there. Not where we could easily find them."

"That means we'll have to find a way. Though I feel like that's all I've been saying." He practically shouted the words, and I knew he wasn't the only one in this room tense enough to break.

"We're going to keep searching and, honestly, get ready for another attack. If you hurt them the way you said you did, they're going to be angry. They're going to try to retaliate," Steele put in.

Chase nodded. "We know what to do. We'll get there. We'll protect this Pack."

"And tonight, the two of you will rest," Audrey put in as she walked into the house, sliding her hand into Gavin's. "I heard the tail end of that as I was prepping the teams. You two need rest. You need to celebrate your mating, even if just for a moment. We do not have these joys often lately. We'll keep the den safe for the night. And, in the morning, we'll plan the next phase of attack. I promise, Alpha. I'll protect your Pack."

I moved forward, wrapped my arms around Audrey, and she hugged me tightly.

"Love you, Alpha's mate," she whispered, and the words settled into me.

I would be the Alpha's mate. This would be my Pack. It didn't seem real.

Chase moved forward then, cupped the back of Audrey's head, and kissed her forehead. "Be safe. And this is your Pack, too, you know. I trust you with everything."

Audrey smiled, though there was still stress in her eyes. "And the Pack trusts you, Chase." With that, everyone walked out, leaving me alone in Chase's home.

In my future home.

Because I was the Alpha's mate.

He turned to me then, his wolf in his gaze. "You were hurt."

I shook my head. "So were you."

"I don't like you being hurt."

"Honestly, I wasn't a fan of it either. How did this happen?" I asked, and both of us knew I wasn't speaking of being hurt.

He cupped my face, then lowered his forehead to mine. "I don't know. I love you so fucking much, Skye. I wanted it to be you. I wanted the prophecy to be wrong and for me to know it was you."

I traced my fingers along his brow. "But the prophecy was *right*. You saw me, and you knew."

"I almost lost you." The words sounded as if they'd been ripped from his throat.

"You didn't. I've been searching for my home forever. And I always knew that I was safe at the Redwoods. That I had a home, people that I would always love and that would always love me and care for me. I knew that. But I didn't feel like I could fully use my wolf until it was almost too late."

"You were always meant to be with me. And I was almost too stupid to realize it until it was almost too late."

I shook my head, gripped his shirt. "No, we just were fooling ourselves thinking we could walk away."

He rested his forehead on mine. "I'll never walk away from you. Though I will push you behind me because I'm tired of you getting hurt trying to save me."

"Let's save each other. For always, Chase." My wolf nudged at me, wanting more, wanting forever.

Patience.

"Are you hurt still?" he asked, his voice deep.

I swallowed hard. "We're both covered in blood and gore, but the Healers did some miraculous things."

He growled, then crushed his mouth to mine.

I knew that we needed to formulate a plan, meet with the other wolves, and speak with my family. There were so many things that we had to do. This war was just beginning, and the Pack needed to see their Alpha, to make sure he was alive, but Chase was a man and a wolf in that moment. Not an Alpha. He was mine. And we needed to prove that to each other.

He picked me up, and I wrapped my legs around his waist as he carried me back to his bedroom. We walked past his bed, into the bathroom, and then we were in the shower, the water spraying down on us. He pulled off my borrowed sweatshirt and his borrowed sweatpants, clothes that Gavin and Steele had given us when they had come to save us.

I knew that other teams had gone in different directions, but the Tracker had been the one to find us, as only fate would allow.

The Pack had saved us. Had found us. We would always do the same for them. And I would always do what I could for this Pack. But first, I needed my mate. I needed him to know that I was his.

He kissed me hard, both of us naked, wet, thrilling.

Dirt and blood slipped off of us as we washed each other, taking it slow, exploring each other's mouths as we gasped in air, needy for one another. My wolf was aching, needing her mate. I could feel his wolf dance along our fragmented bonds, not fully there because we weren't fully mated yet. But close enough that the magics between us were doing weird things.

"Once I mark you, once I bite you, you're mine. You're Aspen. You're the Alpha's mate, with all the responsibilities, magics, and life that comes with that. Are you ready?"

Water slicked over both of us as I smiled wide and cupped his face. "I've been waiting for you all my life, Chase Leyne."

"I feel like I've been waiting for you my entire life, Patricia Skye Jamenson Anderson," he whispered, naming all of my names that made me roll my eyes.

In answer, he crushed his mouth to mine again and picked me up, gently, since we were still tender, and pressed me against the back of the shower. He slid into me softly, both of us taking our time. He explored my breasts, and I slid my hands down his back, gently scraping my nails but not breaking the skin.

It was an easy loving. We had done fast and hard and angry and sad. We had done everything before and would continue to meet each other where we were until the end of our days because this was forever, an eternity.

This was my mate.

We had already completed this part of the bond, but I needed to know that he was alive and mine. So when he kissed me again and moved his mouth down my throat, I tilted my head to the side and felt his fangs scrape against my skin.

"Mark me. Make me yours."

He growled low in his throat, the sensation going straight to my nipples where they were pressed against the crisp hairs of his chest. And then he bit down, and I let out a gasp, orgasming right then and there, clamping around his cock as he bit down hard. Blood scented the air, but it wasn't something to remind me of the death and pain of before. Instead, it was hope and future and mine. He slid his fangs out of my neck, licked the wound closed, and then he was turning slightly, and my mouth was on his. We kissed hard and achingly, the bond between us flaring, but not complete, not yet. My wolf howled, and I knew what I needed to do. I went to his neck and bit down, letting his groan fill the air as he pulsated hot seed deep within me. We both came again and again as the bond snapped into place.

I could feel his darkness, his pain, his weakness, his strength. This was a man who had sacrificed everything over and over again for his Pack. He had hidden those trials and tribulations because he hadn't wanted them to see what they had cost him.

But I knew. And the Pack needed to know.

Only, what if they already had?

I could feel his worry that the Pack didn't trust him, but I knew that they did. I knew that they saw a man they believed in. It wasn't him that they didn't trust. It was the past that lay broken in temptations and darkness.

We were stronger. I felt all of that through the bond. Each time I took a deep breath, the lines that brought me into the Pack strengthened. I was connected to every single Pack member. Far away and close by.

Whether they lived in the den or outside it. Whether they were dominant or submissive or maternal. If they were shy or verbose or strong or weak. Those broken and whole, those mated and not. Everyone who was Aspen was within me. The bonds that brought me closer to the hierarchy, to Audrey and everyone pulsed, and I felt them reaching out to me, welcoming me as their Alpha's mate.

I wasn't Alpha, but I was his touchstone. Their touchstone. I was the protector, their balance.

I was Chase's. And he was mine. And, as I looked up at him, I knew that no matter what came at us next—and it would be coming quickly—I would fight to the ends of the earth for him. For my Pack. Our Pack. For our past and our future.

I kissed Chase again, and I knew the hunt was on.

CHAPTER
TWENTY

Chase

Our moment to breathe and enjoy our mating was over before we could blink. We slept hard for two hours, our wolves needing to rest, our bodies sore from everything that had occurred in the past few days. Neither one of us could allow our minds to drift for too long because the vampires were coming. We knew that. They had been following us since we had escaped, giving us a reprieve only to get inside our heads.

So now I stood with Skye, both of us dressing for battle as we knew they had to be on their way.

"I can't believe I'm an Aspen now," Skye said softly.

I looked up at her, and my wolf pushed, just slightly, wanting to be near her. I couldn't yet, not when I knew if I touched her in any way, we would be stripped naked, enjoying our mating once more. I had to be stronger than that, even though I didn't feel quite strong enough.

"Are the bonds too much?" I asked. "I don't know how an Alpha's mate works." I frowned. My mother hadn't been a typical Alpha's mate. Not with what Dad had done to her, so I didn't know what mantle Skye would be holding within her...if any. Each Pack was different, and Skye was far different than any other wolf I knew.

Skye frowned, came up to me, and touched my face. My wolf bucked at the reins, but I held him back, knowing that I needed to be stronger than my own urges and desires.

"Your father hurt your mother and most likely found a way so she couldn't be the Alpha's mate that she needed to be."

I loved how she could seem to read my mind without me having to utter a word. I nodded. "That's what I was thinking as well. I'm not quite sure exactly what was done because my mother was gone when I was very young. I barely remember her."

"I'm sorry." She kissed my jaw and my wolf relaxed slightly.

"I don't know what happened to her other than she

was murdered by him. Blade hadn't always been the man that he'd become. He hadn't always been a murderer and a power-hungry thief. But I think time and circumstance and his own greed turned him into the monster he was." I turned away, needing a moment. "I feel like his legacy will always be here, no matter what we do as Aspens. The world will see us as the traitorous Pack, and me as Blade's son."

I hadn't meant to say that part out loud. We didn't have time for that, but it had weighed on me for so long, and I could keep no secrets from Skye. She was my everything. From now until forever.

Skye just scowled at me as she turned my face to her. "You carry guilt, I know. But you also have a Pack who loves you. You see distrust in the gazes from everyone because you know they're scared. But they're not scared of *you*. They're scared of the coming war, and they were scared for so long under Blade's reign. But it wasn't your reign."

"You know what that elder said." I'd told her of the elder's distrust, of her as well, and she had scowled and raged, but in the end, she was stronger than me.

"No. We're not doing that, Chase. That elder was wrong. *Is* wrong. And he'll see it. But honestly, Chase, what if he's just as scared? Scared of what Blade did, but not frightened of what you could do. There's a difference. And I hope you realize that. This Pack needs you.

I can feel their bonds. And I don't feel fear of you or distrust of you. They love you, Chase. They see what you bring the Pack. I can *feel* it."

"Skye."

"Don't Skye me. You are who they need. And I will show them that I'm who they need, too. You say I'm a Gamma? Well, let me be one. Let me level you, calm you. Let me find a way for you to see that this Pack loves you, because they do. I saw it before the bonds, and I will feel it forever after.

"I love you, Chase. I won't let anyone hurt you, especially not your Pack. But I truly don't believe they will. Let go of your guilt. Breathe."

I lowered my head to kiss her but froze as Cruz shouted from the distance.

"Chase, they're coming."

I cursed under my breath, smashed my mouth to hers in a quick and ferocious kiss, and then we were making our way outside and running towards Cruz's voice. He was on the northern end of the den property at the edge of the wards, a scowl on his face.

"How many?" I asked, as our soldiers and lieutenants were doing what they were trained to do, get into position, ready to defend the den. The maternals, submissives, and children were all going to their discreet locations, ready to be evacuated if needed. We had a plan. We trained for this. It was what we did, and yet I hated that our den was under siege once more.

"I'm not sure, but at least a hundred."

I cursed under my breath. "We have more, but I don't want to use all of us."

"What about the Redwoods? The others?" Skye asked from my side.

Cruz nodded at her. "We have some of their sentries here, too, since we knew that the attack would be here. Everyone's alert. And it's not like we're literally next door. It's at least an hour's drive for some of them."

"Okay. Where do you need me?" Skye asked, my pride in her flowing down our bond.

"By my side."

"You better not go out there and try to protect me the whole time, Alpha," she growled.

Cruz's lips shifted into a smile as he looked between us. "This is nice. It won't just be me yelling at him for endangering himself just to let everyone else stay unscathed."

I scowled at my Heir and mate. "I'm not sure I like the two of you ganging up on me."

"Get over it," they both said at the same time.

Cruz cleared his throat. "Skye, you can be with patrol A, as you've been training with Audrey and Adalyn."

She nodded. "Good. I'll still be in reach of you. I

promise. Don't get hurt." She kissed me again, then moved towards where Audrey was getting ready.

"Hell. This isn't how I wanted to spend the day after my mating."

"No, I wouldn't think so," Cruz whispered. "You know, sometimes I wish I could just go back to a time where I was just working for the construction arm of our Pack, working on the business end of keeping our Pack afloat. But now here I am, ready to fight right alongside you."

"Fuck," I growled.

"Pretty much. But we will fight. We always do."

I looked at my Pack, some within the den wards, some outside along with me, and I growled low, getting their attention.

"Remember who we are. *Pack*. Protect our den, our people, and yourselves. Remember their magic, but know you're stronger." I threw my head back and howled, the others joining me in a beautiful crescendo that soothed the beast within. Some were in wolf form, others in human form. Hayes had turned into his large polar bear self, far more vicious as an over thousand-pound bear. He roared along with our growls and howls, and my wolf kicked in, ready.

"Give up now, wolf, and we'll take it easy. We just want your Alpha." Valac walked out as if he were here for a business meeting, though he was strapped to the nines in blades, Sunny by his side, a red catsuit the color of blood. She winked at me, her face scarred from Skye's claws.

I grinned and met my mate's gaze for an instant before I looked back at the pair.

"We've hurt you before. We will again. I'm tired of you coming onto my land." My wolf snarled, and I let my gaze glow gold.

"It won't be your land for long."

"Let's get to it. I'm bored," Sunny chirped, and then the vampires were moving, a wave of fangs and claws and snarls.

I howled once, my patrols doing what they should. We met them in the field, claws and fangs against claws and fangs. I cursed under my breath, hating the fact that I might lose people today. But I couldn't think about that. Instead, I had to do what I could to protect every single person I could.

It didn't matter that everything hurt, that my Pack was in danger once again. We would prove to these vampires that they didn't get to come after us again.

The first vampire came at me, and I slashed down, going to my knee to punch up through the vampire's chest.

Others were fighting on a hill nearby while Audrey, Adalyn, and Skye fought as a unit, the three women having trained together for so long, it was as if they had been doing it their entire lives. They each had weapons, as well as their own claws, and were taking down vampires one by one. Some of the vampires were mindless drones that were fighting just to taste blood. Others were sentient, using all of their skills as fighters against my wolves.

There were some vampires that were standing back, the controllers of those without thought.

I knew that Steele was getting closer to them while he protected Wren at his side. Wren would go to any wolf that hit the ground and use her Healing powers, Steele there to protect her.

Hayes slammed through crowds of vampires, his large claws slicing through them like butter. Wynter, surprisingly, was following him, gun in hand, as she took down others that he missed or shot them directly in the head to make sure that they were down for the count.

With that big polar bear as her protector, nobody would get near her. She wore a bulletproof vest and a helmet, and though she was human, she was still out there on the field, protecting her Pack. She had trained for this.

We all had.

Other humans were out on the field as well, all soldiers and lieutenants.

Lily and Dara were ahead of the wards, holding hands as they chanted, their magic pulsing. They kept the wards together and tried a new spell that would inhibit any personal wards made from the vampires. Other witches from other Packs and witches who lived in the city and weren't associated with the Packs nor the coven were there as well, each taking strategic places around the dead. We didn't know if this would work, but it was in our plans. We had trained. We were doing our best.

Gavin and Cassius were fighting together across the field, each of them in charge of their units. They were fierce fighters and knew what they were doing.

Cassius' mate, Novah, was within the den wards, weaponed up and ready to protect the young in her care. She might be a latent wolf, unable to shift, but she was a fierce fighter who could take down anything in her path if the vampires got through us and the wards.

Cruz was at my side, the two of us taking down vampires as we moved towards Valac and Sunny. They were protected by a circle of vampires, but we would get closer to them.

There wasn't another option.

Other wolves were fighting, all of them doing their best to protect our den and our people. This was only the beginning. And I refused to let it be anything else. We needed to make this an ending. Seamus, our submissive wolf sheep-farmer, was out there, fighting alongside Ronin and Dorian.

The three of them were a unit, and even though Seamus was a submissive wolf, he was still a damn good fighter. The dominance of your wolf didn't matter much when it came to protecting your Pack.

Dorian hit the ground, a vampire at his neck, and I growled and jumped, flinging the vampire to the side. Dorian, the one wolf I knew who distrusted me, looked up at me, his eyes wide.

"Thank you, Alpha. Thank you. We have to do this. You're right. I trust you. Just protect us. Like you always have been."

Stunned, I let Ronin and Seamus pull the elder wolf back and then I moved with Cruz, all of us trying to get towards the den.

Lily let out a scream as a vampire came at her, and Cruz cursed under his breath.

"I have to go protect them. Their wolf is down."

We had had two wolves protecting Dara and Lily, and one was bleeding from the side, the other down, unconscious. I could still feel them along the bonds. I sent as much energy as I could, and I knew Wren was on her way.

I nodded tightly, and he ran off toward Dara and Lily. I kept moving in the direction of Sunny and Valac, and when the vampire leader looked at me, he grinned.

"It's about time we finished this," the vampire general snarled.

He lashed out, and I ducked underneath a punch before slicing him in the gut. The vampire winced but kept coming at me, both of us using our skills to get one another. Valac was strong, possibly even stronger than me, but he didn't have the passion I did, didn't have the people to protect. He threw his vampires out like cannon fodder.

I would not do that to my Pack.

Out of the corner of my eye, I saw Audrey fall. Gavin shouted as he went towards her. Others were hitting the ground but getting back up, bloody, torn, but we were *winning*. Only, if we didn't take out Valac or Sunny, they would come at us again and again.

I knew that the demon behind all of this was important but, for now, it was these two that were the priority.

Skye was there then, fighting hand to hand with Sunny, a fierce determination in her gaze that I also felt down the mating bond. She wanted revenge for what Sunny had done, and I didn't blame her. But I refused to let her get hurt.

However, it wasn't in my power to stop her. She was fierce, a fighter. She could do this.

And I had to pay attention to the vampire in front of me.

Valac snarled. "You think that Malissa was the only one? The only one we had within your ranks? How naive of you to think. We have more than you'll ever know."

Traitors. Valac had more traitors within us? I hoped to the goddess he was lying, because our Pack couldn't take another traitor, not with everything we'd gone through.

"I'll find them if you're telling the truth," I snapped. "We always do. But you're lying. You're pulling at what you think you need to in order to rock us. You'll fail like you always do."

A powerful magical pulse hit then, and Dara screamed, agony slicing through my bonds. I looked, and Cruz was on the ground, his eyes wide, blood seeping from his mouth.

The bonds that tied us together as Alpha and Heir fluctuated as if he were gone, but...*not*. And then Dara's eyes went black, and magic pounded the air, the deafening cacophony of terror and darkness.

Everyone hit the ground at once, the magic sliding into our skin something foreign and...evil.

I scrambled up, my ears ringing, and Dara lay on the ground next to Cruz, both of their chests moving. I had no idea what the fuck had just happened, but I would find out. But I couldn't pay attention to them just then.

I needed to focus on Valac. The vampire punched out and I clawed the man in the face, growling. "Get off our land. You'll never be stronger than the Aspens."

"You fool. We already *are* stronger. The world will know who their masters are, and it was never the wolves."

I needed to end this and protect my Pack. My people were dying, and this couldn't be dragged out any longer. "We never ruled. We lived, we survived. That's all we want. You're insane."

"Of course, you would think I'm insane. But it won't matter,"

I punched out, but before Valac could say anything else, I clawed the other man down the side. Valac didn't even flinch as I nearly gutted him, blood oozing.

Then I saw what Valac was looking at. Sunny was on the ground, and then Skye was there, blood covering her, and I felt her rage and fear and anger and hope all twined down the mating bond. She met my gaze for an instant, and I nodded tightly as she brought the sword down over Sunny's neck, and the vampire woman screamed, a sharp shriek before a loud silence filled the field.

Valac roared and magic shook the ground. The vampire's personal wards, the wards they had been trying to use this entire time, burst, slicing out at all of us in a rush. As Dara was passed out and Lily on the ground next to her, I knew the magic had overwhelmed all of us. All of us Aspens were flung to the ground, feet away from where we had been standing earlier.

"Chase!" Skye screamed, and I shoved myself towards her, crawling as I fell again, Valac's rage and magic quaking the earth.

Sunny's head lay at a distance from her body, blood covering the ground in a sticky red puddle.

The other vampires looked up at Valac in fear, and as Valac turned to pick up his wife's head, I cursed and moved to Skye's side.

"Skye!"

"The bitch is dead, but oh my goddess," she muttered through a bloody mouth that matched my own.

Valac howled, and then vampires echoed their leader's sound before retreating in a deafening rush.

I stood there covered in blood, wounds, aches, and I looked at my mate, my mouth wide. "What the fuck just happened?"

"I think Valac just lost his mind," she whispered, her eyes wide in shock.

I crushed my mouth to hers for an instant before I looked around at my Pack, to see who we lost, to see who we ended.

I didn't want to know. I wanted to go back to a time when they all would be whole and healthy, but a good Alpha would fight and bleed for his Pack. And he would face the horror of what he found.

There were people on the ground, Wren and her

team moving from person to person. I knew that rein-forcements would be there, that we'd be able to clean this up. The blood wouldn't stain the earth for long.

But I knew we hadn't come out of this unscathed. I had felt some bonds between me as Alpha and them as Pack break.

I looked over at Cruz, who sat up, rubbing his head, Dara's pale body lying next to him, and wondered what I had missed.

Dark magic had seeped into the air and the earth today, but I didn't think it had been only Valac who had done it.

I didn't have time to think about that. My Pack needed me. And we might have won the battle, but the war was far from over.

CHAPTER
TWENTY-ONE

Chase

My wolf paced as I walked through the hallways of the infirmary, doing my best to help Wren and her team wherever I could.

Skye was doing the same, though this was her first official day as the Alpha's mate. We hadn't had a ceremony yet. The moon goddess hadn't fully blessed us under a full moon, but our bond was strong, and the Pack could feel it.

We had sentries from several Packs, including ours, stationed around our den, and we would do the same for the other Packs when needed. But now we were the

271

ones hurting, with Sunny dead and Valac raging. That meant another attack could come at any moment. So we were on alert. Waiting. And healing.

Skye stood next to Lily's bed, holding the younger witch's hand as they had a quiet conversation. I could hear fragments of what they were saying, and I knew Lily was trying to reassure my mate that she would be okay.

"Lily, rest. You fought well for your Pack. Wren will be able to heal up this cut soon, and you'll be right as rain. You are a beautiful and soulful witch. I'm so proud that I will get to know you more."

My wolf preened at the way that she protected our Pack. She was doing what an Alpha's mate should. Hell, she was doing more than some would.

Melanie, the Redwood Alpha mate; and Brie, the Talon Alpha mate; and now Skye, seemed to have even more power and attentiveness to the den than others. They were strong and were Alphas in their own right.

I was damn proud.

"You okay, Chase?" Steele asked as he walked toward me.

He had a bandage on his arm, and I knew the cut had to have been bad if he was still wearing it. Steele usually refused medical treatment. But here he was, protecting those he could.

"I'm fine. A few scratches, but somehow I ended up

mostly unscathed." My guilt ate at me, but then Skye appeared, scowling at me.

"Stop it. You have been hurt beyond reason in every other altercation. This time you were one of the lucky ones to hold strong for us. You have bled for them today, every other day you can. It's okay." She cupped my face and I lowered my head, letting my wolf show her that I adored her.

Steele cleared his throat, and I noticed everyone was staring at us.

"Well. At least we know what the Alpha's mate can do." He winked as he said it, then went over to Hayes.

The big polar bear Omega sat next to two injured soldiers, speaking to them in growling, soft tones. They would be okay, but they had been seriously hurt. It would take longer for them to heal. I could sense warmth sliding out of the Omega and icy coldness sliding back in. He was leeching away their fear, not all of it because everybody needed their own feelings, but he was doing what he could to decrease the intensity of it.

"Where else can I go?" Skye asked.

I looked down at her, but it was Audrey who answered. "Help me hold Adalyn down so I can splint her leg."

Wolf on alert, I turned when Skye did.

Adalyn snarled. "I don't need to be held down. I don't even need a splint. I'm fine."

"Your leg is broken, and while I can use my Healing powers to help, I need to conserve what I can. Plus, since it's broken in two places, it will be better to let it set as it is. It won't take long, and you won't be in a cast for long, either. Please, stop." Wren put a little more of her wolf into her voice, filling me with pride. She might be slightly submissive, but she would meet the gaze of any wolf in her care.

"You guys are mean," Adalyn said with teary eyes. I didn't know if it was pain or anger, probably a little bit of both. But Skye went to hold down her friend, along with Audrey, as Adalyn had her bones set.

Dara lay still and unconscious, and Cruz looked like he had gone through hell and back. He stood next to her bed, scowling down at her, and I had questions about what had happened with them. I could still feel him down the bond as Heir. He held the mantle to soothe the responsibility and burden that Skye and I had, but something was wrong. And I was going to have to figure it out eventually. Cruz needed me and I'd do what I could for him.

"Excuse me," a small voice said from beside me, and I turned to see Alexandra, another elder wolf who had fought on the battlefield next to us.

"Alexandra, is everything okay?" I wrapped my arm around her shoulder, and she nuzzled into me.

She was a fierce wolf who was slightly dominant and had been a maternal wolf before Blade had ruined everything.

"We love you, Chase," she stated, her voice full, clear. I froze as everyone around us continued to work, but all ears were on us.

"Alexandra..." I began.

She put her finger to my lips. "No. We are the elders. Your team, the core, is here. The maternals are here, the children are safe where they need to be, with their parents or with those there to protect them, but they know this, too. *We love you, Chase.* When you were a boy, and we couldn't help you, we loved you then. We have always trusted you. I know that you thought differently, and maybe some have been wrong, but they've learned. They've seen you. Be our Alpha. Know we fight beside you. We did so today. Thank you for being our Alpha. Thank you for putting your life on the line countless times. For your mate for doing the same," she said as she looked over at Skye, who now cried softly.

I swallowed hard, my wolf quiet for the first time in a long while as we digested her words. "We are one. I know we are." I looked over at Skye, who gave me a thumbs up. I nearly rolled my eyes but knew I needed to be serious for now.

"We have to be one. We've had to for a long while." I looked into the gazes of so many, even those who ducked because their wolf wasn't strong enough, but I wanted them to know that I was there for them, watching them, that this needed to be said. Finally. I needed to get my head out of my ass and say it. "We have to look to the future, not the past. I know what my father did, more than most," I said, as others whispered, pain radiating along the bonds.

Hayes stood up, held out his hands, and the emotional bonds that tethered us as a Pack began to ease. I didn't know how he could do that all at once, but he was taking it into him, just enough, so we could breathe. The pain was unending, yet soothing with Hayes around. I gave him a grateful nod and continued.

"I love you all as mine. I am your Alpha. I will earn that title until the end of my days. We are Aspen. We are part of the alliance. And we will be here. No matter what. Just know that I will always be there to help you. We might not know what's coming next with the vampires and with the humans. But we will do what we can. Just as we always have. We will learn, we will train, and we will fight. And along with that, we will live. We will have matings, children, we will learn. We will grow our businesses. We will *thrive*. We will not hide behind our wards and pain and secrets. The world knows who most of us are, and they won't shy away from us. So we won't shy away from the world. No longer will we hide where we are because of fear. It's time we grow like the other Packs. That we trust in who we are as Aspens. It's time we show the world who our Pack is. And that, no matter who comes at us, we will fight. Because we are one. We are Aspens."

Skye came to my side as I spoke, held me close, and then the howls began. Pained howls, mournful ones, and ones with pride. We would still need to heal, we would still need to fight, but we would live.

No more shadows, no more darkness.

———

I KNEW I SHOULD PROBABLY BE WITH MY TEAM, BUT this was one thing that they didn't need to be part of. Skye knew where I was, and of course, Steele would because he always did. Cruz and Audrey as well because they were my Pack, and they always had their eyes on the rest of the Pack.

I needed to have this meeting as was always promised.

I thought back to promises and prophecies, I knew that sometimes those could be twisted and read incorrectly, but right now, that didn't matter. I went to the neutral zone, as we called it, and got out of my car, the sound of my feet on gravel the only noise in the forest, prey and predators alike quiet with the sense of so much power.

Gideon, Kade, and Cole stood there, speaking to one another, arms folded over their chests. There was no aggression, no need to see who was dominant. No, we were four Alphas, meeting for a private discussion.

Yes, we could do this over the phone and include the other Alphas from around the world, but for now, we liked to be in person. Our wolves needed it.

And frankly, so did the men.

"You're late," Kade said as he raised a brow.

I shrugged. "We've been a little busy."

"I'm sorry I wasn't there," Cole put in as he squeezed my shoulder. "A new baby was born, a new little pup ready for the world. Their Alpha needed to greet them."

I grinned then, the idea of new life thrilling me. I hugged him tightly, slapping him on the back. "Congratulations, Alpha."

"I feel like a proud pop myself even though he's not mine," Cole said with a laugh as Kade and Gideon both congratulated him on the new pup.

"We should also congratulate you," Gideon put in, and my wolf preened again.

"It's been an eventful couple of days," I stated, before I went into detail about the attack, the kidnapping, and the vampires.

Gideon's gaze clouded over while Cole began to pace. Kade just gave me a look. "We'll have to talk about Skye."

"She's my mate," I bristled.

"Damn straight she is," Kade added with a laugh. "But she is also a Redwood. There are strings," he said with a laugh.

I tensed, but Gideon was the one who barked out another laugh.

"Good strings, but strings," the Talon Pack Alpha added.

Considering Gideon was mated to Brie, another Redwood Pack princess, I figured that he would know.

"We must protect our people," Cole said after a moment. "Our Packs are diverse in our strength, in our powers. And I know we're coming together. But there must be a better way, magic or not, because while the vampires have their attentions on the Aspens, I feel like that's only the beginning."

I nodded at the Central Alpha. "You're right. It is. Valac told me that we were the beginning, that I was the first prize they wanted before they got to the rest. So we will fight together. A true alliance, for the moon, with the moon goddess herself."

We looked at the crescent moon and then down at the ground before letting one claw slide out of our fingers and slice through our palms. We looked at each other, nodded, and blended the blood of four Alphas, the magic pulsing out of us in a woosh.

It wasn't a bond, it wasn't a joining of Packs, but it was a promise.

One made under the sliver of a moon, with blood and bone and bond.

We were one. We were a Pack.

And it was time for the world to know it. But, until then, I would go back home to my mate and begin the next phase of what it meant to be Aspen.

CHAPTER
TWENTY-TWO

Valac

VALAC STORMED THE OFFICE, HIS CLAWS RAKING down the books in front of him. Others milled about, and he knew they were talking about him. He knew that they were worried. But they didn't matter. None of this mattered.

It felt as if his heart had been ripped from his chest, torn asunder as it burned.

"Valac."

Valac whirled towards Neg, glaring. "Get out."

"You're hurt. Let me clean up the blood. Then we can kill the Aspens."

Valac reached out and slashed his claw across Neg's chest. Neg stood there, the demon in front of him raising his chin.

"I'll let you do that once. Once. Because Malphas asked. But do not think that I am your lackey."

"I'm fine. Let me be. I'm fine."

Valac heard the nonsense in his tone and knew he would lose his mind if he weren't careful.

Neg left, and Valac wondered if he would see him again. Because Neg and the other demons rarely came here. At first, it had only been Malphas, the only demon who was here to be their master. Their only master. And yet Malphas had his own plan. A plan that had been set in motion long before Valac had been turned.

Sunny had been turned with him. He roared, her name a broken whisper on his lips, and turned to the mirror, his eyes wide.

"I need to make a plan."

His third came up to him, another vampire with catlike eyes narrowed.

"Let's get you cleaned up. We need to clean the wounds, and prepare for the next phase. You know Malphas has plans. With her. And with the other one."

Valac whirled. "And what of my Sunny?"

"We will avenge her. Just like we have avenged all those who have fallen."

Valac's chest ached as he breathed in and out, trying to control himself.

He rubbed his temples, letting out a breath. "We'll destroy them. But perhaps there's another way. And not with the one that they think."

The vampire in front of him smiled.

"I believe that's what Malphas was thinking."

It should worry Valac that this vampire was speaking to their master so easily because that was Valac's and Sunny's job. But Sunny was gone. Someone would have to take her place as second. Someone would have to avenge her alongside him.

Malphas needed them to be strong, as the demon was twisting its magic on multiple planes.

"If we are careful, we should be able to fight them on a new path. Not at the forefront like we have been. But from the side."

"The Aspens aren't the only Pack here," the other vampire whispered.

Valac nodded as he let the other vampire heal his wounds, something only Sunny had done for so long. "Another Pack. A smaller one. One connected to the Aspens."

"The seeds have been sown, but we can continue," Valac whispered.

The Aspens would learn what it meant to touch a vampire's mate. And they would burn.

They would learn who they trusted had been their own worst enemy all along.

They would know the seeds had been sown long before the Aspens had become who they were. Long before Blade and the goddess and whatever other magic they believed in changed them.

They had killed Valac's mate. And now they would die. For there was no other way. He would hunt them. And the darkness would come, and they would burn. Beginning with the weakest, or perhaps with the Alpha himself.

Only, which Alpha would die first?

CHAPTER
TWENTY-THREE

Skye

"DID YOU PACK ENOUGH UNDERWEAR?" MY MOTHER asked, and I nearly dropped the box I was holding, laughter spilling out of me.

"Really? I've packed all the underwear I own. You know that."

"It's probably not enough since she doesn't wear any," Brendan said, and I flipped him off.

"Shut up. I wear underwear. You're just being weird."

"Stop talking about this. I'm done," my dad said as he held up his hands. "I'm trying to help you pack up

285

your house so you can go move in with your mate over an hour away in a new Pack. Suddenly my baby girl is with the Alpha of the Aspen Pack as if the world hasn't rocked off its axis."

"Oh, Daddy," I said with a laugh as I held him close.

"Don't call me that. That's what you call me when you need something."

"I just love you. Okay?" I looked up at my strong dad, who looked the same age as I did because wolves didn't age, but there was a sense of responsibility and knowing about him. Because he had seen hell and had come out through the worst of it with my mother and created our family.

"I love you, Dad."

"Don't make me fucking cry," Logan Anderson growled before he kissed the top of my head and held me close. "Now, let's load up the truck, and then we'll see you off so you can drive alone to your den like you're a freaking adult or something."

"She's not driving alone, remember, Adalyn's here."

"Where *is* Adalyn?" I asked.

"Flirting with Nico," Brendan said as he looked down at his phone.

I snorted and shook my head before taping the final box closed.

"Are they courting?" my mom asked, and I dropped the box.

Laughter spilled from my lips as my siblings began to laugh. "Courting? Courting was an old word when you were a kid."

"I know. It just seemed like a good word. I didn't want to say flirting or banging."

"Please stop," my dad said as he picked up the box from the floor and carried it outside.

Wiping the tears from my eyes, I looked over at my mother. "And I don't know what she and Nico are. I'm pretty sure it's just friends."

"We *are* just friends," Adalyn said as she came forward, a bag of food in hand. "Nico's mother just handed me snacks. That's why I was there. She wanted to say hi. I was not canoodling with Nico."

"Ooh, canoodling, that's a good word," Mom said as she hugged Adalyn tight. "You two drive safe. I'm just sorry that Chase couldn't come."

I nodded tightly. "The Alpha pair can't be out of the den at the same time right now. Not with us on alert." My wolf stood proud at the word Alpha, and with the gleam in my mother's eyes, I knew she felt the same.

Adalyn cleared her throat, took the last of the boxes, and left the house, leaving my parents and me alone. My dad stood by my side, arms folded over his chest, and my mom cupped my face.

Mom cleared her throat. "I'm so proud of you. Not just because of what fate put before you, but what you have put before yourself. You are brilliant, a fighter, and I know that you will know that the Redwoods have your back no matter what happens. Your family has your back. The Aspens are lucky to have you, and I know that as Alpha—Alpha's mate—you will *thrive*. You would've thrived anywhere you went, but now? This is your purpose. And I've never been prouder to be your mother."

Full on crying now, I wrapped my arms around my mother and held her tight, as Dad hugged both of us.

"I love you, baby girl," he growled gruffly.

"I love you both. This isn't like I'm moving out of your house. I haven't lived with you guys for a bit now." Why was I crying like this?

Mom let out a watery laugh. "But you're all mated. And the mating ceremony's coming up, and there's war, and okay, this is too much. I need you to go now so I can cry in peace."

"I'll hold your mother while she cries. Don't worry. She won't be alone."

I looked at my parents, two people that loved each other and their children beyond measure. And I knew that they were the template from which I had been cast. And they were the promise I made. I said my goodbyes, hugged my brothers tightly, and waved at my cousins, even though I knew I would see them soon. We were one alliance now, and with technology, the speed which it took to get from one place to another was almost nothing. I would see them often, and I would fight by their sides. But for now, my new Pack was waiting for me. My mate was waiting for me.

Adalyn and I snacked on empanadas in the front seat as we drove to the den, my wolf prancing inside, waiting to see her mate. Adalyn just laughed as I jumped out of the car and threw myself into Chase's arms as soon as we drove onto the den lands. We weren't even near the Alpha's home, *my home*, but I needed Chase.

"I was about to run out and get you. You were gone too long," he growled before crushing his mouth to mine. People whistled and hollered, but I ignored them, needing my mate.

"I'm sorry it took so long. Adalyn drove like a bat out of hell at least, so it didn't take longer."

My friend cleared her throat. "You know it. I'm driving the car all the way to your home. You guys can walk, take your time *canoodling*," she added, and I laughed, shaking my head as she left, Lily jumping into the front seat with her. I shook my head and held my mate, feeling sad at the loss of my past but knowing that my future was paved in promises.

"Come on, Audrey promised dinner at the house."

"Audrey's cooking?" I asked.

"No, Gavin is, and Cruz is helping." There was

something in his tone at Cruz's name, and I frowned at him.

"What's wrong?"

"I don't know. Adalyn has been more surly than usual, though I'm glad the cast is off, even though it was only on for a few days. But Cruz? I don't know. I think that will hurt us more than the fates are letting on. I just don't know it all yet."

I frowned and tangled my fingers with his as we made the journey to our home, stopping to speak with Pack members along the way. Chase was loved, and I was glad that he finally saw it. When Pack members came to me to ask questions, congratulate us on our mating, and just hold me, a new surge filled me. I felt like I could be part of this, too. That it wasn't just Chase that could find love and strength in a Pack. I didn't know how to be an Alpha's mate. I had never had it on my radar before. But I had seen how the Redwood Alpha's mate had reacted and grown. I saw how Brie did it with the Talons. I could find my own way, but I knew I had the best examples and support I could in this place I was in.

We walked inside, and the entire hierarchy was there, along with a few familiar faces as people laughed and put my neatly labeled boxes into the rooms they belonged. I smiled, realizing that I was moving in with my mate, that this was our future. We were together, *forever*, bonded and mated. And as we took the time to figure out our daily routines and traditions, they would be *ours* as we grew into them. We'd make our path and know we'd always have each other.

I knew it might be wrong to some to think about a future and happiness and mating ceremonies when everything was going to hell around us. At the same time, the real threat of vampires and demons and the unknown were over our heads at all times. Yet Chase had been right when we had been in the infirmary. We needed to focus on what we held, as well as on our futures. On our day-to-day and growth, so we thrived as Aspens and wolves and shifters instead of being on the alert at all times.

I listened in and gave opinions as we went over the classes that some juveniles needed to take, including martial arts and archery and sharpshooting. There would be hiking classes and mountain climbing within the Pack. Farming and ecological and technological growth. Some Pack members would be moving back into the city, no longer needing to be within the den wards because we would not hide. Blade had done that to them, not Chase, and now people were finally feeling safe to do so. Things were changing, and we were finding a way to work.

Dara, who looked quiet, a little sad, spoke during dinner after clearing her throat. "I've been speaking with Hannah and some of the other witches, and we might have an antidote to those dark black shards of magic, but we won't know until the next fight."

I froze before I sat up. "The magic that sank into my skin and altered my wolf?" That's what had been coating the dagger when I was stabbed what felt like ages ago.

Dara nodded. "Yes. And some of the magic that we used seemed to work against the wards partially, but it took a lot of energy. I think almost too much." She coughed. "I'm fine," she added when every single dominant looked over at her.

"Drink this," Cruz scowled as he handed her a glass of water. She nodded in thanks, but the two didn't touch. I glanced between them, wondering what was upsetting my wolf, but I couldn't put my finger on it.

"We're working on it. And I hope to find out more soon. I have a couple of contacts across the country with different witches, covens, and some circles that had nothing to do with our current coven," she said, her voice a little bitter.

"Good. Any help you need, I'm there," Adalyn added. "I don't like the fact that I was hurt like I was. So, let's kick some ass."

"On that note, welcome to how our Pack works," Audrey said as she held up her glass for a toast. "Skye, welcome to our Pack. We're a little wild, but we like food, we like each other most of the time, and we're Aspen. We're figuring it out, one stumble at a time."

"I think we should get that embroidered," Wren said with a laugh, and Hayes threw his head back, shocking me at the sound of his deep and beautiful laughter. I leaned into my mate, looked up at him, and smiled.

When my phone buzzed, as did the others, we looked up, and Steele scowled, flipping on the TV behind us.

"And as you can see here, in breaking news, the vampires, yes, you've heard that right, *vampires* have come out from hiding. We don't know how they're connected to the shifters themselves, but as you can see, this vampire has killed a human being and has declared war on society. We now know that vampires are real. What else is hiding in the darkness?"

I looked at my mate and knew that things had just gotten harder.

CHAPTER
TWENTY-FOUR

Cole

I had been an Alpha for around as long as Chase had, and yet for me, it felt as though I was an amateur while Chase fought the vampires in battle after battle.

I looked down at my hands, knowing I needed to be stronger than this. Needed to be better. I was the Alpha of the Central Pack.

It always made me laugh inside when Chase mentioned that he was the cursed Alpha, the one who was trying to clean up after his father's sins.

The Aspens hadn't lost their magic. Hadn't been

relegated to nothing. Hadn't lost all forms of bonds and blessings from the moon goddess herself.

No, that had been the Centrals. That had been *my* people.

I stood at the entrance of my small den, knowing that we didn't have the hustle and bustle of the others. We lived and worked outside the den most times because there just wasn't enough space. It was safer for us to blend in with the humans rather than keep all of our people in one place. Or maybe it was because we had always blended in before we had become a den, and it was harder to leave that practice.

My wolf pawed at me, knowing it wanted to run, to see someone.

But that wasn't an answer.

My wolf wouldn't allow them to be the answer.

I needed to focus on my Pack, the powers that weren't strong enough, and the fact that the Aspens needed us to be at their side. What would happen once they realized that we were not the Pack that they thought we were? We didn't bring anything to the table except our hearts and whatever power we had. The Talons and the Redwoods were the ones with all the strength. I felt as if we were failing.

I shook my head and knew I needed to be better. Chase had learned to believe in himself, so damn it, I could too.

Because we weren't a large Pack, it was my turn to be on patrol. We guarded the small territory between the Redwoods and the Talons on the north side of the neutral zone. And since it was my turn to be on this side of the land, I was nearest to the Redwoods, and our paths crossed more often than not.

So that was why I scented him.

The person that I shouldn't.

It was odd because Nico was nearly my age, but I felt so much older than him. He was the son of the former Healer and a human, and a wolf. The son of the Redwood triad, the legendary power base that had brought honor, respect, and hope to the Pack itself.

And there was something special about Nico.

Something that angered my wolf.

Just like someone else angered my wolf.

But an Alpha didn't get to think those thoughts, and I had to remember that.

I turned the corner, knowing that we were probably on patrol together. Nico and Skye often ran together, but I knew she was healing, and now her patrol would be completely different since she was the Aspen Pack Alpha alongside Chase.

I still couldn't believe I hadn't guessed at her powers. Of course, I had never met someone like her before, having only thought it was a bedtime story, not something that could be true.

But there were so many surprises in that family, *in all of us*.

It was a surprise to everyone that I was the Alpha. I shouldn't be. But here I was, and there was no going back now.

"Are you getting all grumpy again?" Nico asked, grinning up at me.

"I'm not grumpy." I growled the words, sounding grumpier. "Shit, I can't help it. I was thinking."

"If that's what you think," Nico said with a laugh. "You in the mood to run?" he asked.

"Honestly, yes."

"Sounds good to me. I would say things have been a little quiet here, but that would be a lie."

"And bad luck," I growled.

Nico just shrugged, and we began our run in silence since we needed to keep our senses tuned in to the area around us. I was a strong wolf, could shift faster than most, but Nico was fast in general. The magic that he used was a thing of beauty. And sometimes, it took me a lot more than it should to stop staring at him while he moved. I wanted to think it was just admiring his magic, but now my wolf had other ideas.

"Hey there, you guys," another familiar voice said and we both stopped, Nico nearly tripping over his feet, very unlike him.

Adalyn stood there, a smile on her face as she waved

at us, Lily by her side. Adalyn was an Aspen Pack hunter, a beautiful wolf who could fight like nobody else, and Lily was a witch of the Aspens, with barely any power, but used everything she had to protect her people.

They were our friends, but it was odd to see them up here near the Central den.

"Hey there, Addy, Lily. What are you guys doing here?" Nico asked.

Addy? Since when did he call her Addy?

And why was I jealous?

And *who* was I jealous of?

"I'm just escorting Lily here to meet with the Central Healer," Adalyn answered as Lily waved.

"Yes, there are a few things we're going to go over book-wise, and Adalyn wanted to drive." Lily beamed at us, and the four of us stood there, on attention since we were still on patrol, but it felt good to be here, to talk to them.

But my wolf was confused.

Just like the rest of us.

"Are you guys on patrol?" Lily asked.

"We are," Nico answered easily. "Do you want us to escort you to the Central den?"

That should have been something I said since I was the Alpha, but I didn't mind Nico speaking since he was better at it, and my tongue seemed to be tied. Something odd was going on, and my wolf and I didn't like it.

"We're good," Adalyn said. "But if I see you on my way back, I'll join you. I'm off for the day, but I could still use a run."

My wolf pushed at me to say something. Anything. "Just keep an eye out. You know why."

There I was, grumpy and growly again.

Adalyn gave me a look Nico seemed to share, and Lily just looked confused.

"Is everything okay?" Adalyn asked.

But I didn't have time to answer. Instead, Adalyn's eyes were wide, and then Nico was growling, and I was throwing myself over the three of them, Lily's scream echoing in my ears.

There was a flash of light, a shrill voice, heat, a burn, and then nothing as a bomb went off in the middle of exactly where we had just been standing.

Next in the Aspen Pack series?
Find out what happens to Cole, Adayln, and Nico in
MATED IN CHAOS

WANT TO READ A SPECIAL **BONUS EPILOGUE** FEATURING CHASE AND SKYE **CLICK HERE!**

A NOTE FROM CARRIE ANN

Thank you so much for reading **HUNTED IN DARKNESS!**

This book was years in the making. Chase...Chase I knew. He was Alpha. He was ready. I NEEDED to write his story.

Skye? She surprised me. But why wouldn't she, considering her parents and grandparents.

This book is for the scene I wrote a decade ago that broke me.

This book is for you.

Next up? It's time for a menage romance! People wanted a Central Pack series and while I'm not ready to write that kind of series, I was ready for the Alpha. Cole, Nico (A Redwood), and Adalyn (An Aspen), are waiting in Mated in Chaos!

The Aspen Pack Series:

Book 1: Etched in Honor

Book 2: Hunted in Darkness

Book 3: Mated in Chaos

Book 4: Harbored in Silence

And if you're in the mood for a paranormal romance outside the world of the Aspens:

The Ravenwood Coven Series:

Book 1: Dawn Unearthed

Book 2: Dusk Unveiled

Book 3: Evernight Unleashed

WANT TO READ A SPECIAL BONUS EPILOGUE FEATURING CHASE AND SKYE CLICK HERE!

If you want to make sure you know what's coming next from me, you can sign up for my newsletter at www. CarrieAnnRyan.com; follow me on twitter at @CarrieAnnRyan, or like my Facebook page. I also have a Facebook Fan Club where we have trivia, chats, and other goodies. You guys are the reason I get to do what I do and I thank you.

Make sure you're signed up for my MAILING LIST so you can know when the next releases are available as well as find giveaways and FREE READS.

Happy Reading!

ALSO FROM CARRIE ANN RYAN

The Montgomery Ink Legacy Series:

Book 1: Bittersweet Promises

Book 2: At First Meet

Book 3: Longtime Crush

The Wilder Brothers Series:

Book 1: One Way Back to Me

Book 2: Always the One for Me

Book 3: The Path to You

Book 4: Coming Home for Us

The Aspen Pack Series:

Book 1: Etched in Honor

Book 2: Hunted in Darkness

Book 3: Mated in Chaos

Book 4: Harbored in Silence

The Montgomery Ink: Fort Collins Series:

Book 1: Inked Persuasion

Book 2: Inked Obsession

The On My Own Series:

Book 1: My One Night

Book 2: My Rebound

Book 3: My Next Play

Book 4: My Bad Decisions

The Promise Me Series:

Book 1: Forever Only Once

Book 2: From That Moment

Book 3: Far From Destined

Book 4: From Our First

The Less Than Series:

Book 1: Breathless With Her

Book 2: Reckless With You

Book 3: Shameless With Him

The Fractured Connections Series:

Book 1: Breaking Without You

Book 2: Shouldn't Have You

Book 3: Falling With You

Book 4: Taken With You

The Whiskey and Lies Series:

Book 1: Whiskey Secrets

Book 2: Whiskey Reveals

Book 3: Whiskey Undone

The Gallagher Brothers Series:

Book 1: Love Restored

Book 2: Passion Restored

Book 3: Hope Restored

The Ravenwood Coven Series:

Book 1: Dawn Unearthed

Book 2: Dusk Unveiled

Book 3: Evernight Unleashed

The Talon Pack:

Book 1: Tattered Loyalties

Book 2: An Alpha's Choice

Book 3: Mated in Mist

Book 4: Wolf Betrayed

Book 5: Fractured Silence

Book 6: Destiny Disgraced

Book 7: Eternal Mourning

Book 8: Strength Enduring

Book 9: Forever Broken

Book 10: Mated in Darkness

Dante's Circle Series:

Book 1: Dust of My Wings

Book 2: Her Warriors' Three Wishes

Book 3: An Unlucky Moon

Book 3.5: His Choice

Book 4: Tangled Innocence

Book 5: Fierce Enchantment

Book 6: An Immortal's Song

Book 7: Prowled Darkness

Book 8: Dante's Circle Reborn

Holiday, Montana Series:

Book 1: Charmed Spirits

Book 2: Santa's Executive

Book 3: Finding Abigail

Book 4: Her Lucky Love

Book 5: Dreams of Ivory

The Branded Pack Series:
(Written with Alexandra Ivy)

Book 1: Stolen and Forgiven

Book 2: Abandoned and Unseen

Book 3: Buried and Shadowed

ABOUT THE AUTHOR

Carrie Ann Ryan is the New York Times and USA Today bestselling author of contemporary, paranormal, and young adult romance. Her works include the Montgomery Ink, Redwood Pack, Fractured Connections, and Elements of Five series, which have sold over 3.0 million books worldwide. She started writing while in graduate school for her advanced degree in chemistry and hasn't stopped since. Carrie Ann has written over seventy-five novels and novellas with more in the works. When she's not losing herself in her emotional and action-packed worlds, she's reading as much as she can while wrangling her clowder of cats who have more followers than she does.

www.CarrieAnnRyan.com

CPSIA information can be obtained
at www.ICGtesting.com
Printed in the USA
LVHW091045300822
727116LV00013B/425